THE BILLIONAIRE'S PRINCESS

FAIRY TALE BILLIONAIRES

AVA RYAN

1

DAMON

SHE GLIDES in like the queen of everything without bothering to notice the fancy Friday night crowd here at Bemelmans in the Carlyle Hotel on the Upper East Side. Forget about making eye contact with anyone or acknowledging the pianist plinking away on the grand. The server gets a nod of thanks as he seats her at the leather banquette against the wall at one of the small round tables nearest where my brothers and I sit. A hint of a dimpled smile as she accepts the menu. Then the server walks off and she lowers her eyes to study the drink selections, retreating into a cool bubble of aloofness that only the brave would dare try to penetrate.

I am nothing if not brave.

Don't get me wrong. *Brave* is probably not the first word people use to describe me. *Ruthless* comes to mind. As do *arrogant*, *brilliant* and *rich*. Generally followed by the word *bastard*.

For example? *Damon Black is an arrogant bastard.*

Not that I care what anyone thinks of me. You don't bring your late father's floundering property development company back from the brink of disaster and turn it into a billion-dollar-ish real estate empire by the age of thirty-four by tiptoeing around people's feelings.

But *her*...

I notice everything about her, oblivious to my brothers' ongoing conversation and too riveted to bother lowering my dirty martini all the way back to the table.

The pale skin and vivid auburn hair that seem to distill and concentrate the room's rosy glow on her sleek face and swelling cleavage. The way the spaghetti straps of her little black dress skim her kissable shoulders. The graceful neck and the way a single gleaming corkscrew strand of hair escapes her severe bun and trails down her back. The way her long and shapely legs culminate in pretty feet that feature pink-tipped toes strapped into killer heels.

No rings on her left hand. A funny detail I usually don't care to notice one way or the other but that now gives me a surge of satisfaction that I plan to pretend I don't feel.

She studies the menu. I study her, my skin prickling with awareness as I experience the slow curl of desire in my belly and lower.

"Damon?"

The thing is, this is new for me. Not noticing women in bars, obviously. I notice women. I hook up with women. But lately I do both with all the enthusiasm of a man brushing his teeth before bed. My body needs it and it's got to get done. I may as well get it over with as quickly as possible so I can move on to more important things. My boredom, which teeters on complete indifference most of the time now, is a hazard of the singles scene here in the city as much as my chronic workaholism. I'm not excited by too much of anything these days, except for the huge deal my brothers and I closed this afternoon.

Wanting someone to screw is not new for me.

Wanting anyone the way I suddenly want ye olde ice princess over there? Brand new for me.

I don't believe in romantic love. Let's put that out there right now. My parents blasted the idea out of my head and left a crater for my heart when they savaged each other during their divorce back when I was ten. I jeer at friends who fall "in love." But a woman like *that*? I can understand how she'd put a crazy thought or two into an unsuspecting guy's head.

"Damon? You with us?" one of my brothers asks.

"Shut the hell up," I say mildly without ever looking away from her, ignoring their round of sniggering at my expense as best I can.

The server delivers the woman's martini and slips away again. She looks up suddenly, possibly feeling the weight—or maybe the heat—from all my focused attention on her face. She looks across at me, and our gazes connect. I freeze and do my best to overcome the sensation of landing flat on my ass and having the wind knocked out of me.

She's insanely gorgeous. Huge eyes with sweeping brows. Oval face. The kind of plump berry mouth that'll make a plastic surgeon rich quick around these parts.

I watch as she freezes like I just did. As her mouth opens into a surprised little O. As a telltale blush originates across the tops of her breasts, creeps north and settles in her high cheeks. As her expression cycles through surprise and subtle feminine appreciation before ending in an unmistakable flare of annoyance that makes her lips thin.

My glass continues to hover somewhere near my mouth, so I raise it to her in a toast and die a thousand tiny deaths while I wait for her reaction.

She hesitates, clearly thinking it over. Then, to my utter astonishment, she flashes the beginnings of a sexy smile that promises heaven on earth between her legs. My heart pounds and pounds harder as she stands and shimmies her clingy dress into place with some delightful hip action. My mouth waters, I admit, and keeps watering when she picks up her drink and takes a couple of steps in my direction. My floundering brain recovers enough to order me to stand and greet her, which I start to do. I should mention that I usually prefer to do the hunting, but this works for me. If you're out deep-sea fishing and a swordfish flops onto your boat and lands at your feet, you don't throw the thing back, do you? No. You don't. I'm also usually low-key about these interactions, but there's no stopping my thrilled grin from its complete facial takeover.

Until she stops on the other side of her own little table, lobs a withering frown in my direction and sits facing the banquette she just vacated, presenting me with her lovely back. Leaving me stunned and seriously disappointed.

Like a fucking loser.

My brothers guffaw while I linger there, half up and half down.

"That one's going to leave a nasty bruise in the morning." Griffin, my thirty-two-year-old middle brother, claps me on the back in a mock show of sympathy.

"You're going to want to ice it down before you go to bed *by yourself* tonight."

He's right. I snort back an involuntary laugh as I sit again, rubbing my aching chest under the guise of straightening my tie.

I feel dazed. No shit.

She got me. I'm man enough to admit that. She's got beauty and a sharp sense of humor. I like that. A lot. I'm also betting that she can run pretty hot for the right man.

I *am* that man. I *will* be that man. Tonight, if I can help it.

She can sit there with her back to me all she wants, sipping her martini while congratulating herself on her cleverness. Let her enjoy her brief victory. The poor thing doesn't know that she just took my smoldering fire for her and poured a million gallons of gasoline on it.

But she'll learn.

"Want me to show you how it's done?" says my thirty-year-old youngest brother, Ryker, jerking his head in her direction and starting to stand. Just like that, a haze of red filters my vision, and it has nothing to do with the ambience here at Bemelmans.

"Sure," I say, reaching up to push him back down again with all the force I can muster. "As long as you're cool with that being your last act on earth."

This kicks off another round of raucous laughter between Tweedledee and Tweedledum, but a bigger problem materializes in the form of a corporate titan wannabe who sidles up to her table with his cheesy grin firmly in place. I watch and wait to see how she greets him, the tinge of jealousy I just felt with my brother now escalating into a wave of bloodlust.

It's probably her date. A woman who looks like *that* doesn't spent her Friday nights alone.

But she stiffens when he steps into her range of vision. Shakes her head when he leans in and says something to her. Speaks loudly and clearly when he persists:

"Fuck off."

I register the throaty sound of her voice and the British accent even as my inner caveman takes the lead and propels me to my feet. Pretty ironic, considering I would've sworn as recently as ten seconds ago that I'm not the jealous type.

A murmur of dissent rises from my brothers as I head in her direction without another word.

"Keep it cool," Ryker calls after me. "We'd rather not have to bail you out of jail tonight."

But I'm on a mission and don't have the time or inclination to reassure him. I'm not sitting idly by while some SOB in a shiny suit harasses my ice princess right in front of me. Can't do it.

"Sorry I'm late," I say, putting a protective arm around the back of her chair and startling them both. Shiny Suit shoots me a glare, but I only have eyes for her and the flare of relief in her expression as she tips her face up to look at me. "Everything okay over here?"

2

DAMON

A PREGNANT BEAT PASSES. I raise my brow at her, proud of my one-upsmanship, but she recovers quickly. The glimmer of mischief in her expression warns me that my triumph will be short-lived.

"About bloody time, Ruprecht darling," she says smoothly. "You know I've been worried about your proctology exam this afternoon. I do hope your bottom will be okay."

I choke back a startled bark of laughter. A ringing relative silence follows. I'm not sure which one of us is more horrified, me or Shiny Suit. The guy actually backs up half a step, as though he expects some flesh-eating germ to leap from my ass to his and wants to maintain a minimum safe distance.

She stares up at me, those clever eyes gleaming with an unmistakable *gotcha*.

I award her several more points before reminding myself that two can play this game.

I hadn't planned to touch her—not yet—but plans change. So I bend and give her a lingering kiss by her ear, savoring both the subtle hitch in her breath and the scent of lavender that clings to her warm skin.

"The only thing I love more than a challenge is a wicked sense of humor," I murmur.

Maybe I'm imagining things, but I detect a tiny feminine hum of pleasure at my touch.

"Don't worry," I say in my regular voice for the benefit of our audience as I pull back. "All of my private parts are in excellent working condition. You'll see later. Make a new friend?"

She sends me a subtle narrowed dagger of a look before focusing on Shiny Suit.

"Not really. Some men see a woman alone at a bar whilst waiting for friends and act as though they're in the buffet line at some horrible cafeteria. You know the type of awful man I'm talking about, don't you, darling?" A pointed look in my direction. "Anyway, this stranger was just leaving. Because I don't pick up strange men in bars."

"Ah," I say, shaking the startled man's hand and putting a hand on his shoulder to steer him out of the way as I ease into the banquette opposite her. "You can't blame a man for trying. Have a good night, buddy."

"I'll do that," the man says sourly, now holding his hand out as though it's been dipped in warm elephant shit.

"Oh, don't worry," I say brightly. "It's not contagious."

The man walks off, muttering darkly and shaking his head. Leaving me alone with a flinty-eyed female who evidently doesn't appreciate my humor.

"I thought he'd never leave," I say. "And couldn't you give me a better name than *Ruprecht*?"

"Why on earth would your name matter when you're about to go back to your own table?"

Something about the throaty voice, upper-class British accent and withering disdain coming from *that* mouth drives me absolutely freaking insane.

I put a hand over my heart and try to look wounded.

"This is my reward for rescuing you just now? Not very friendly, is it?"

"The word *friendly* has never once been used to describe me. I'm happy to buy you a thank-you drink. Once you *fuck off to* your own table."

I laugh. I can't help it.

"I'm glad I made the walk over here. This will be more fun than I thought."

She frowns. "What will?"

"Warming you up," I say, staring her in the face.

Vivid color stains her cheeks. "I do *not* need warming up."

"I disagree," I say with an easy shrug. "I've lost three toes to frostbite since I walked over here."

"Then by all means," she says, her expression stony. "Walk back before you lose the rest. If I'd wanted to be bothered, I'd have sat at the bar. I repeat: fuck. Off."

"If you don't want to be bothered, you need to do something about that face and body. Those *eyes*." My voice gets husky, much to my surprise and irritation. Women fall into my lap. I don't throw myself at their feet and creep along the edge of stalker territory in the slender hope of getting them to smile at me. "And you'd probably stop with the dirty talk if you knew how much *those* words coming from *your* lips in *that* accent turns me on."

Something about my unsmiling delivery of this information seems to catch her off guard. She hesitates, her eyes widening as she opens her mouth and manages to say zip.

We stare at each other, my breath held during the agonizing wait for her verdict. Because I *will* leave if she insists. I won't be happy about it, but I will.

She looks bewildered. Uncertain.

Also unwillingly intrigued and hopeful.

"You're not married, are you?" she finally asks.

"No," I say, deciding not to add that if I were married, I'd lie my ass off about it for a chance to spend the night screwing her senseless.

Something in her expression reluctantly eases. The sight of this softening loosens up my chest and allows me to breathe.

"Felon? Sociopath? Pedophile? Fraudster?"

"Nope." My ears burn. "Just a guy intrigued enough by a woman to stick his neck out a little. Risk making a fool of himself. Which is not something I normally do. Take my word for it."

"Well," she says, her voice somewhat warmer as she breaks eye contact and smooths her hair behind her ear. I'm not going to lie: it's something of a relief to be out from under her high beam. The intensity of the pull I feel toward her when we look at each other is starting to mess with my head. "You've come all this way. A good couple meters from your table. You may as well have a drink. Fuck off immediately after that."

"Works for me," I say, relieved.

We start to smile at each other, but she catches herself.

"As long as you understand that this is just a drink until my friend gets here." She hitches up her chin. Gives me a stern look. "I'm not going upstairs to the hotel with you. Or anywhere with you."

The statement is patently absurd. The electricity is so thick between us that you can almost hear it crackle.

"You don't believe that, do you?"

My curiosity gets the best of me, and maybe her innate honesty gets the best of her. Whatever. I wait, my entire existence poised for her response. She hesitates, her color high as her attention dips to my mouth. That feels like answer enough.

Until a pair of shadows looms over our table, breaking this growing spell between us.

"So much for drinks and dinner with us," Ryker says, automatically turning up the wattage of his toothpaste-commercial smile for the benefit of an attractive female. "Can't say I blame you for ditching us, though, Damon. Want to make the introductions?"

Since I don't want to admit to my brothers that I haven't managed to get her name yet, I decide to start with them.

"The ugly one here is my middle brother Griffin," I tell her wearily, eager to get these two jokers out of the way before they cause any undue mischief. She laughs in a display of flashing white teeth and dimples that makes something swoop inside me. "The stupid one is my youngest brother Ryker."

"Carly." She shakes both their hands in turn. "Pleasure."

Carly.

Even her name pleases me.

"You can do so much better than this guy," Ryker says, jerking his head at me. "Don't you want to reconsider now that you know you have better options? Maybe ditch him and come to dinner with us?"

"No," I say sourly. "She doesn't. Bye."

"I can almost always answer questions directed at me," she tells me. "I'm very proud of that skill. I learned it in primary school."

I scowl. Meanwhile, my brothers nudge each other and grin with delight. I can only imagine the commentary I'll receive from them later.

"But I have promised Damon a drink, boys," she continues. "I'm regretting my decision already, but there you are."

"Ah," Ryker says. "Well, if you change your mind, we'll be happy to—"

"*Bye,*" I repeat.

More laughter at my expense, followed by good-natured waves as they head back to their table, leaving me alone with Carly and a pounding heart.

She raises a brow at me. Represses a grin under the guise of pursing her lips. "Where's my drink? I was promised a dirty martini."

"*I* was promised a dirty martini," I say, signaling for the server to bring us two more.

"Your brothers seem quite lovely."

"They're a nightmare." I throw in a dramatic shudder just to make sure there's no further question of her taking off with one of them. "Between the nose picking and the bedwetting, they've disgraced the family a thousand times over."

She laughs again, this time a full-throated edition that engages her sparkling eyes and dimples.

I watch greedily, trying to remember that this is not my first smile, laugh, flirtation, woman or, God willing, hookup. But feeling my skin sizzle as I try to dial back my excitement, it sure feels like it.

"Christ," I mutter, shaking my head at myself and ruffling my hair with both hands.

She looks bemused. "What?"

I tell myself to slow it down. But the words pour out, unstoppable.

"I've been dying to make you laugh. I thought I could handle it. But that's not a normal laugh. It's been spiked or something. It went straight to my head."

She doesn't know what to make of me. I can tell by the vague frown between her brows and the way she chooses her words.

"Don't bother flirting with me, sir. I already told you it won't work."

"You said something about not fucking me tonight," I say, shrugging. "Neither one of us believed it at the time. Still don't, as a matter of fact."

She glares at me, oblivious to the server as he drops off our drinks and fades into the woodwork.

"You're a cheeky prick, aren't you?"

"You have no idea," I assure her.

"And why would I waste my time with such an arrogant arse, pray tell?" she demands.

I lean closer, dying to touch her as I rest my elbows on the table.

"Careful," I say, giving her a pointed once-over that lingers on her eyes, lips and cleavage. "You're going to want me inside you before the night's over. Don't make it too hard to get yourself back on the playing field."

She makes an outraged sound, her face flooding with color. But before she can let me have it with both barrels, as she clearly intends to do, her phone buzzes on the table. Lobbing a final glare in my direction, she checks the display and scowls.

"Well, this is *brilliant*," she says. "Now my friend Michele's gone and canceled on me."

"Works for me," I say with a cheery toast.

"I'll just bet it does."

"Don't look at me like that. I had nothing to do with her not coming." I pause to reconsider. "Other than hoping and wishing for it."

She rolls her eyes, unable to entirely quash her amusement. That's about the time that the pianist ends his solo set and a new performer takes the mic, introduces herself and launches into a tender and plaintive rendition of "Since I Fell for You." The one thing the setting needs to become even more spellbinding than it already is. I watch her sing the opening few notes, then turn back to Carly.

She levels her gaze on my face. Steady. Smoldering. Expectant.

Honest to God, it's all I can do to think a coherent thought when she looks at me like that.

I open my mouth, my voice on a three-second delay.

"What if we drink our drinks and listen to the music. See where the night takes us. Can we do that?"

"Yeah," she says softly. "We can do that."

"Good. Come sit with me. So you don't have to crane your neck."

I slide her drink over to my side of the table, and she follows suit, easing into the banquette on my right side. I shift closer, taking care to brush my leg against hers.

"This is better, isn't it? Easier for you to see the singer this way," I say.

As if the singer is remotely on my mind at this moment.

"Make yourself comfortable," Carly says dryly, looking a little startled.

"I will. Thanks."

With that, I wrap my arm around her waist and pull her even closer. I leave my hand right where it is when I'm done, somewhere between waist and belly and not that far north of her pussy. She feels solid. Warm. Vibrant. Thrilling. To my immense pleasure and surprise, she covers my hand with hers, lacing our fingers together. I kiss her bare shoulder in response, noting the way she gasps and helplessly turns her head toward me. As though she hopes I might accidentally kiss her lips before pulling all the way back.

But I don't. I sit there holding her and listening to a voice so evocative and beautiful that it makes my nape prickle. Maybe the martinis have been stronger than I thought, because for one wild second I think that I could live and die in this moment. Then it occurs to me that I'd rather die with her legs wrapped tight around my waist and me buried to the hilt inside her.

So I use my free hand to take *her* free hand and raise it to my mouth for a lingering kiss. And when I'm done with that, I lay her hand on my thigh, palm up, and trace letters while we listen to the music.

I.

W. A. N. T.

Y. O. U.

She ducks her head and grins, curling her fingers around mine.

"Look at me," I murmur, tapping her chin to make sure she does as I say.

She does, reluctantly, her glittering eyes taking up my entire field of vision at this close range. I wonder again what color they are, but there's time for that. I'll find out later.

"If you don't want me, now's your chance to say so," I tell her.

"You know I want you," she says, much to my profound relief. I didn't think she'd admit it so easily. "But I never do this sort of thing."

There's only one possible response to that.

"What you and I have done before is irrelevant to what you and I are going to do with each other tonight."

Her eyes unfocus as she thinks this over, then zero in on my face once she decides.

"And what's that?" she asks, a soft and secret smile curving her lips.

I stare at her for a beat or two, lost.

Swear to God, I am going to fucking eat this woman alive.

"You're going to wait for me in the lobby while I book us a room upstairs," I tell her. "When we get up there, you're going to let your hair down so I can see it. You're going to let yourself go and have fun with me. You're going to be a tiger. All night. And I'm going to do my best to make you come harder than you've ever come in your life. No questions asked. No regrets." I pause, giving my words time to sink in. "Deal?"

A subtle but delightful shiver runs through her.

"Deal," she says.

3

DAMON

I GET A SUITE, humbled and unpleasantly surprised to discover at this late stage of both my dating and professional lives—I'm thirty-four and have a net worth that has eight zeros before the decimal point—that I am not above throwing my money around to impress a woman I want. But she's worth it because she has both intrigued me and made me laugh, two things no woman has done in longer than I care to remember. Why take chances with this overwhelming feeling of excitement that seems so determined to tackle me to the ground? Why not do everything I can to make sure she sticks around for a while?

The registration process seems to take forever, especially because I keep one eye on her where she sits over in the lobby waiting for me. Half of me fears that she'll bolt if I let my guard down and look away, but she seems patient. Possibly even as determined as I am. And when the key is in my hand and I give her a look, she meets me at the elevator.

We stand side by side, anticipation humming between us.

The doors slide open. We step inside, blessedly alone. I press the button and retreat to one side, where I lean and shove my hands deep into my pockets, not trusting myself to touch her yet. For one thing, there are cameras everywhere. For another, my self-control dangles by a frayed thread. Unless Superman shows up to help me out in the next thirty seconds, this train will take off once it gets started, and there'll be no stopping it.

She retreats to the other side and faces me, also leaning. Her gaze touches my eyes. Hovers over my lips, which, of course, prompts me to involuntarily lick them. For my part, I notice the way her breath speeds up, making the lush curves of her breasts strain against the front of her dress where it dips. Her dewy mouth. That shiny hair.

Evidently my thoughts are louder than I realize. Without breaking eye contact or smiling, she reaches up and pulls out a pin. Gives her head a little shake. And produces a gleaming cascade of silk with highlights of red and gold, orange and brown and combinations in between in colors I don't know.

With that, she transforms herself from a beautiful woman into a goddess.

I wonder, with a fleeting twinge of despair, why she's here with me when she could do so much better. Then I wonder how long it will take her to figure that out and bail on me.

But she's here now. And I'm not one to question good fortune when it smacks me in the face.

When the doors slide open, she raises a brow at me. I tell her the room number. She leads the way with long, purposeful strides, allowing me to enjoy the stellar view of her tight ass and toned legs. A woman who looks like this is an athlete. Another detail about her—like her last name and country of residence—that I'm determined to nail down and examine at the earliest possible opportunity. As for right now, we're almost at the room, her swinging hair is within easy reach and I have better things to do.

When we arrive at the door, all bets are off.

She glances over her shoulder, shooting me an impatient look. I take my hands out of my pockets and give her the key, freeing up my hands to help themselves to hanks of that fragrant and silky hair at her nape. The strands are long and thick, warm against her scalp, and I can't get enough as I press my body against the back of hers. She lets loose with a hum of approval that accelerates my surging blood. Then she opens the door with steadier hands than mine.

We stagger inside the suite, where I loosen my grip just long enough to shrug out of my jacket, drop it to the floor and flip a switch so we can see where we're going. Then I wrap her up again from behind, my greedy hands seeking out breasts and belly, hips, pussy and everything I can reach in between while I steer her down the hall toward the bedroom and nip her neck, driving her into a frenzy.

She whispers to me the whole time, words and hints of words that are more encouragement than I need.

"Damon."

"Ah, God…"

"Don't stop. Please don't stop. I need your hands on me—"

Her heated response to everything I do drives me out

of my freaking mind. I turn her around when we arrive at the edge of the bed, eager to taste that gorgeous mouth. She's right there with me, already opening as she wraps one arm around my neck and the other around my head. She tunnels her fingers through my hair, standing on her tiptoes and straining to get closer as she scratches my scalp with her nails.

Funny how I told her to be a tiger. I didn't count on her turning me into a mindless animal.

This is no tentative first kiss while we get the feeling of each other. We're both too hot and urgent for that. There's no time to pretend we're not desperate to make each other come. Besides, we fit and move together perfectly. She turns her head the way I need her to. Grants me absolute access to her lush tongue and mouth. Surges and retreats to my rhythm. Wraps a leg around my waist before I can demand that she do that very thing. Moans when I knead her ass and thighs. Lets me go and backs up a step just as I experience the frantic thought that I can't wait another second.

Not one more second.

A long beat or two passes while we stare at each other and try to catch our breath. We're both trembling. The look on her face is an absolute reflection of the way I feel, which is shellshocked.

Shellshocked.

I watch with a wary new respect. It dawns on me that I need to give this woman a wide berth before she does me some serious damage. Less than an hour into our relationship, whatever it may turn out to be, and she's made my hands shake, my mouth dry out and my thoughts scatter. God knows what will be left of me after I fuck her.

Probably just a lump of ruined flesh and a stray pubic hair or two.

It also dawns on me that I couldn't care less. If that's the price I need to pay, then let me grab my wallet and max out my credit cards.

"You're rocket fuel." Shit. Even my voice is ruined. "You know that?"

"Only because you're the ignition switch." She flashes a smug smile. "And I *thought* I heard you say something about playing with a tiger?"

"You should've warned me," I mutter.

"You're a *big* boy." She eyes my crotch, where the world's hardest dick strains for her the way those giant magnets strain for old cars in a demolition yard. "I'm sure you'll be fine."

"I *will* be fine." I undo my belt and zipper. Toe off my shoes and toss my wallet onto the nightstand. Take her face between my hands and give her a languid kiss, teasing her with the slow stroke of my tongue. My reward for managing half an ounce of self-control? The way her head falls back, and her eyes roll closed as she groans. "But that's all the foreplay you get this time. Sorry."

"Thank God," she says, shimmying for me when I reach under her dress's hem to ease her panties down her long legs. "I'm dying here."

"I'll be the judge of that."

I rip the covers back, scoop her up and toss her into the middle of the bed, exactly where I want her. Her squeal of delight thrills me. As does the way she eagerly levers up on her elbows to wait for me.

"Pull your skirt up."

Holding my gaze, she complies by bending one leg,

digging that heel into the mattress and executing a sexy little hip wiggle that's the most riveting thing I've ever seen. Then she takes her time about pulling her skirt up just enough to reveal a glimpse of the manicured patch of hair that proves she's a natural redhead.

"That's enough."

She stops, perfectly willing to let me look all I want.

And what a view it is.

Her pussy is plump and beautiful, glistening with her juices and ready for me. But I trail my fingers through her slick cleft anyway, savoring both her feminine coo of pleasure and my corresponding power over her.

I just hope she never discovers that *she* has the power to make my pulse pound and my throat tighten until it's a wonder I can even breathe.

"Last chance," I say, reaching for my wallet and desperately hoping I have more than one condom inside it.

"I don't want any chances. I want you to hurry up and fuck me."

Just in case the raw need in her voice doesn't drive the point home, she reaches down to touch herself, resuming where I just left off.

I make a sound of utter disbelief. How did I get this lucky tonight? Will I also find a bar of gold under my pillow when I wake up in the morning? I never take my eyes off her as I blindly fumble my way through nudging my boxer briefs aside and rolling the condom on.

Then I grab her hips and yank her flat, exactly the way I want her. I stretch out on top of her and settle between her legs. She eagerly accepts my weight, exactly the way I knew she would. Eagerly helps herself to my ass and digs in with her nails to pull me closer. Eagerly cocks her hips.

I expected her to do all of that, yet she somehow manages to surpass every expectation.

She's fire and magic. And nothing about this interlude is normal or regular.

I grip my dick and rub it back and forth against the hard nub of her clit, lubricating myself with her cream. I take a moment to stare into her shimmering eyes, glazed now with her lust for me, and regret the fact that we're not skin to skin because I was far too impatient to bother with all these clothes.

Next time, I promise myself.

But right now, my entire existence centers on fucking Carly until she can't shout my name hard enough to keep up with her orgasm.

A single hard thrust. Then I'm buried deep inside her.

We both stiffen and cry out, taking a beat or two to adjust. To *breathe.* She arches, her body straining with need and ready to writhe against me.

"I want you to *move,*" she whispers.

"Not so fast, tiger," I murmur, propping myself on my elbows and locking my hips in place because I know it'll enhance her experience. "Why didn't you tell me you were so tight?"

A shaky laugh from Carly.

"*I'm* not the problem. Your giant cock is."

"That's the kind of thing I like to hear," I say, lacing our hands together on either side of her head as I begin to surge.

She immediately moans and wraps my waist in a death grip between her flexing thighs, her features twisting with gathering ecstasy. She's my perfect match, meeting me thrust for thrust, groan for groan and kiss for endless kiss. She murmurs incoherently but urgently, driving me higher. She strains against me, smiling, laughing and teasing.

She blows my fucking mind.

And then she warns me—"I'm close; I'm so *close*"—before going rigid and letting loose with a single high note of astonished pleasure. An unabashed cry that will surely have our neighbors up and down the hallway cracking their doors open and poking their heads out to see what the commotion is all about.

I laugh as she rides it out, triumphant as I nip the side of her neck and elicit another sexy mewl from her sweet mouth.

"Next time I want to hear my name, tiger."

I glimpse her sated smile.

"Next time, I imagine you'll kill me outright," she says, slapping me hard on the ass to get me going again.

What's a guy to do?

I speed up, pumping my hips with an abandon that makes our flesh smack and threatens to throw out my back. I make guttural sounds that suggest some sort of zoo animal has possessed my body.

I lose myself in her, letting the rapture tackle me to the ground and pummel me into submission.

I shout her name as I come and come and *come*.

It takes a while for me to catch my breath and for the aftershocks to wind down, but that's to be expected following an earthquake that's broken the Richter scale. I reluctantly pull out and stretch out next to her. When it's all said and done, we lie facing each other, more dressed than undressed, legs twined as we stroke each other's faces and, for my part at least, wonder what the fuck just happened here.

I trace her eyebrows. Her nose with its sprinkling of freckles that I hadn't noticed before. The tender cupid's bow of her lip.

She runs her thumb over my cheek and jaw, a slight frown grooving down her forehead. Fun fact: she looks as satisfied yet vaguely bewildered as I feel.

I open my mouth, determined to get a few things straight from the get-go.

That she is surprising and unexpected.

That there is—or could be—something here between us.

That I hadn't planned on anyone crash-landing into my life like this, but that plans change.

Above all?

That we both agree that we're not done with each other.

Not by a long fucking shot.

But no words come.

Even so, she answers my searching gaze with a steady warmth that makes me wonder how I ever thought she was frosty. Then she tightens her hold on my face. Brings me in for a gentle nuzzle of a kiss.

"I know," she says drowsily. "I know."

I drift off with a lingering smile, my head full of plans for more sex during the night, a room service breakfast and leisurely shower in the morning and dinner tomorrow night, confident that she *does* know.

Which is why it's such a horrific shock when I wake up to a cold bed and an empty suite.

I bolt upright, going from dead asleep to jarringly awake in half a millisecond.

"Carly?"

Nothing.

The sickening lurch in my gut tells me the truth. But, stupid MF'er that I am, I try again.

"Carly?"

More nothing. A more emphatic nothing.

I get up, visit the bathroom and do a quick lap around the suite, half hoping to find her passed out drunk behind one of the sofas or some such. At least then she'd be here, and I'd have some sort of explanation that doesn't make me feel like shit.

No such luck.

The truth hits me slowly by degrees, probably because I'm desperate not to see or acknowledge it. But first, I run several increasingly wild scenarios through my mind, trying them on for size. Maybe she ran out for ice. Except that our suite has ice and she wouldn't have needed to take her purse for an ice run. Maybe she meant to leave a note but couldn't find a pen or paper. Maybe a sudden and dire problem with her eyesight prevented her from seeing the pen and paper on the nightstand next to the bed.

But she didn't even bother to scrawl her phone number in lipstick on one of the mirrors.

She left. She's gone. She's not coming back. I'll never see her again.

In that crushing moment, I'd almost rather believe that a crack team of foreign agents extracted her from the room while I was asleep and plan to hold her for ransom. Anything but the truth.

But the truth is that she walked out on me.

Walked. Out. On. Me.

Another woman has walked out on me with zero warning, and *I'm* the fool that's surprised.

Haven't I learned this lesson already? Didn't my mother tattoo it onto the empty space where a heart should be when she walked out on her husband and three young sons to be with my dad's richer best friend? And then again when she got herself killed in a car accident before we could reconcile? This is what women do. They lull you into a false sense of security and then they disappear from your life with no advance warning. They pretend to have a connection with you, then they rip the rug out from under your unsuspecting feet and leave you to try to figure out how to get up again.

I have temporarily and foolishly forgotten this one crucial fact about women.

I won't forget again.

I seethe for a minute or two, plotting next steps.

My relentless and determined side demands that I hire an investigator to start downstairs at Bemelmans and track her down like bloodhounds after an escaped criminal. Her crime? Making me feel like shit.

But my pride won't let me chase her. If she doesn't want me, that's her loss. Like Beyoncé says, Carly's replacement will be here in a minute. Fuck Carly.

Fuck her.

I try to focus on my anger, but my hurt refuses to sit down and shut up.

My brain refuses to accept the idea that that was all of Carly I'll ever get. I'll never have the pleasure of seeing and feeling her pillowy lips wrapped around my dick while she sucks me off. I'll never get to taste her pussy or discover the color of her nipples. I'll never see her smile again or laugh with her again or find myself on the wrong end of her tart humor again.

That was it. One and done.

I rub my hands over my face, laughing bitterly at my own stupidity. But what can you expect from a fucking loser like me? *I* just had sex for the ages, and *she* couldn't even be bothered to give me a fake phone number and pretend she wanted me to call her tomorrow. *I* just spent the better part of five large for this suite to impress her (I didn't become a near-billionaire by wasting money), and *she* was so impressed that she didn't even stay an hour or, hell, try to steal my credit cards.

The worst part?

I know, deep in my gut where it counts, that I can march around impotently cursing her for the rest of the night, but all she has to do is show up again, smile at me and issue some sort of half-assed apology—*any* sort of apology at all—and I will sign up to be her fool again. Whenever she deigns to reappear and crook her little finger at me, I'll be her puppet. I know I will.

Fucking Carly No-Last-Name.

Honestly, walking out is the best thing she could have done for me. I'm glad I'll never see her again.

I mean it.

Glad.

I don't lose control of my feelings like this.

Not for *anyone*.

4

CARLY—THREE WEEKS LATER

YOU'RE NEVER GOING to see him again, you bloody idiot, I tell myself as I hurry down the steps from my apartment building and toward the limousine idling at the curb. *It's all for the best that you take this time to get your life together rather than hang any foolish romantic hopes on some bloke who just wanted a quick fuck. So stop looking for him in every crowd.*

Excellent advice that my roving gaze ignores as I quickly scan the passersby on the sidewalk, hoping for a glimpse of Damon's tall frame, broad shoulders and sleek sable hair. God, I'm so unbelievably stupid. As if he somehow discovered my last name and went to the trouble of tracking me down to my apartment here on the Upper West Side because he couldn't bear the idea of never laying eyes on me again. As though I made *that* much of an impression on him when I know in my heart of hearts that he probably woke up, discovered me gone and said a fervent prayer of thanks that he'd executed a perfect one-night stand with all of the great sex and none of the morning-after awkwardness.

Please, Carly.

Try to muster a single milligram of common sense.

Yet I can't help looking for him. Straining for some sign that he still exists and that I didn't imagine the entire interlude.

But there's no sign. There never is.

To make matters worse, I'm stuck attending some stupid cocktail party for Manhattan's elite, making small talk with people I don't know or care about and trying to pretend that my mood isn't foul when I'd much rather be home reading one of my Agatha Christie mysteries. And the icing on top of my ruined evening? My escort for the night is my father, who made the long flight across the pond from London to "come see his poppet," when we both know that the real purpose of his visit is to rub noses with said elite and to give me shit about the deplorable state of my personal life since my graduation from NYU a few weeks ago.

The chauffeur hops out, races around the car and opens the door for me before I can dream of doing it myself.

"Thanks," I say, gluing a smile onto my face and keeping it there as I slide onto the seat next to my father, his Royal Highness Prince Edmond, the Duke of Montgomery.

Let the fun begin.

"Hello, darling," he says, every silver hair in place as he beams at me and pulls me in for a kiss on each cheek. "How's my poppet? You look lovely. Love the suit. Very smart."

"Thanks, Daddy. How was the flight?"

"A nightmare," he says, then sips his drink as the car pulls into traffic. My attention automatically goes to the rearview mirror, where I see his security detail follow us in a dark SUV. A hazard of being the youngest son of the Queen of England. "Whiskey?"

"Am I going to need it for this conversation?" I ask tiredly.

"Probably," he says, reaching for the decanter.

"Hmmm." I stare out the window—still no sign of Damon; in a city of eight million people, you'd think there'd be *something*—and wait for the official lecture portion of the proceedings to begin. "I can hardly wait."

"I don't understand you, Charlotte." He passes my drink, which I sip gratefully. Perhaps if I burn my throat to cinders, I'll be excused from having to explain myself. "Breaking your engagement at the very moment you're supposed to be moving back home and settling down? Leaving London again and hiding out here before any of us can talk sense into your stubborn head? Ignoring my phone calls for three weeks and forcing me to fly over here for a face-to-face? What's gotten into you?"

I sigh. "I don't expect you to understand."

"I *don't* understand. You and Percy have been together since you were old enough to date. You got engaged last Christmas, right on schedule. Mummy signed off on it. My office have been ready to announce it for months. Yet you tell me to sit on the news. Then you tell the poor chap you need a break. Whatever *that* means. Now *this*. You've gone and ended the engagement entirely rather than ending that ridiculous break."

He finishes his drink. Pours another one.

"Yes, well, I told both you and Percy that I needed a moment to process things—"

"The time for processing is *before* you say yes," he says.

"Is that so? It seems to me that the time for second thoughts is *before* one engages the divorce lawyers."

He grimaces at me.

"Why should there be any question of a split?"

"Oh, I don't know. Maybe because you and Mum had the world's nastiest divorce when I was little. As have several members of the family, come to think of it. Mostly because that ring on my finger started to feel like a tiny handcuff and I couldn't see myself spending the rest of my life in the dull English countryside with Percy. The entire idea made me, I don't know, seize up. Once I realized that, I didn't want to string him along."

"Well, now you've returned his ring and broken his heart. Disappointed me terribly. Does that matter to you?"

"Of course it does. I feel terrible about it."

I revert to a glum stare out the window. I still cringe every time I remember that final conversation with Percy three weeks ago. The way his bright happiness slowly turned to disbelief, quickly followed by horror and, finally, heartbreak as he realized I intended to make our break permanent. I remember his initial refusal to take back his ring. His insistence that we could work things out and that he planned to wait for me. My insistence that we couldn't and he shouldn't because I want to make my life here in New York City.

Not my proudest moment, admittedly. Percy is a great person. One of my oldest friends and my first love. All that means something to me. He deserves someone who will fall passionately in love with him. Who will live for his smile and count the seconds until his return. Who can't wait for the adventure of marriage with him.

None of that is me.

The whole truth?

Percy bores me to tears. There's no challenge. No excitement. And I don't just mean the wild initial phase of sexual passion, although God knows *that* could have used some work. I mean that there were no surprises. I never held my breath to see what he would say or do next. Why bother? I always knew exactly what he would say or do next. Percy has no career ambition. No driving hunger to make something of himself. No need to bother with that, either. Not when your father is an earl worth close to a billion and all you need to do to come into your own fortune is to outlive him.

As for me? I can't wait to get out there and take my bite out of the world. To make my way. To challenge myself and see what I can do and learn and *be* with my painting skills.

How will I manage that? No bloody idea. Yet. But figuring it all out is part of the challenge.

The idea of spending my life on Percy's drafty country estate, popping out children and carrying picnic baskets to his weekend polo matches, sounds like a diabolical form of purgatory.

Still, I completely understand Percy's bewilderment. The poor man is the same today as he always was. It's not his fault that it took me this long to realize that his steadiness and reliability are no substitute for excitement and desire. But can't you have both in a marriage? Shouldn't you want both?

Not that I know anything about marriage, clearly. My most intimate example is the way my parents scorched the earth between them on their way to their divorce decree. I'm no expert. But I'm quite sure that the idea of spending the rest of your life with your fiancé shouldn't fill you with dread. I'm quite sure that's a bad sign.

So, yes, I'm sorry I hurt Percy. But am I sorry to have narrowly avoided the worst mistake of my life?

Fuck no. I'm relieved. *Relieved*.

"How terrible do you feel?" my father asks hopefully. "Perhaps you lovebirds can still work it out."

"I'm not in love with Percy. Not the way I should be."

"Oh, *that*." He flaps his hand dismissively. "Romantic love is wildly overrated. Other things are so much more important."

"Exactly. Like common interests. Understanding. A true *connection*—"

"Financial security."

There it is again. One of my father's vague references to financial concerns, which is quite odd, considering that his mother the Queen is personally worth upward of a billion pounds. He's made these sorts of comments several times in the last few months. I've also heard faint rumblings about my father's debts—the tabloids have referred to a gambling issue—but I've always assumed they were lies generated to sell newspapers and magazines. Now I have to wonder.

"What are you on about, Daddy?"

His expression sours and his movements turn choppy as he helps himself to another drink and downs half of it before answering. My anxiety level grows.

"My beloved brother is tightening the purse strings on *my* branch of the family," he says bitterly. He and his older brother, the heir, share all the love that Churchill no doubt felt for Hitler during the Blitz. "Mummy's not doing anything to stop him. We're all going to feel the pinch very soon. I'd rather hoped to have a wealthy son-in-law as a buffer while we get things sorted."

I gape at him, my mind spiraling through all the things wrong with those few sentences. I hardly know where to start.

"He's cutting us off?" I ask, my stomach dropping as I think about my allowance, which allows me to live and travel comfortably while I plan my next steps.

"Not yet. But the writing on the wall couldn't be clearer."

I breathe a little easier. "I'm sorry it's coming to this, but I'm planning to work for my keep, and I'm sure you'll figure something out. And I'm not some sixteenth-century princess to be married off to form some advantageous alliance. Kindly remember that."

"Of course, poppet. I'm sure you'll be tripping over career opportunities very soon with your degrees in, what was it? Art history and studio art."

"I'm a painter," I say, stung. "I can *paint*."

"It's all fine to set up a studio in one of Percy's barns and dabble on the weekends," he says darkly. "How you think you'll pay the rent here by *painting* is beyond me."

"Thanks for those stirring words of confidence and support," I say, feeling my self-esteem shrivel like a man's willy after a dip in an icy swimming pool. Because he's right, of course. I majored in art because I love it. Not because I ever expected I'd have to support myself with it. "Can't tell you how moved I am."

"Sorry, poppet." He softens immediately and leans in to peck my cheek, his breath pungent with alcohol. I wonder how much he's been drinking these days. "There will be some heavy hitters in the art world there tonight. A discreet word or two to the right people and I can sell several pieces from my private collection. Build up something of a war chest for both of us when times get tighter."

As an art lover, this idea makes my heart sink, but I can't blame him. What else can he do? As a full-time working senior member of the royal family, he can hardly send out his resumés and sit for interviews. At least *I* can get a job as, I don't know, a restaurant server or something if I need to.

"That sounds like a good plan."

"Still…" He chooses his words with delicate care. "I am very fond of Percy. I don't see why you two can't let cooler heads prevail. Talk things through. You young people grow and mature as you get older. Why not grow together? And It's not as though there's some giant obstacle, is there?"

Right on cue, Damon flashes through my mind, leaving me quietly flustered and tingly.

Exactly the way I've been since I first laid eyes on him three weeks ago.

I picture his thick sable hair and the way it falls across his forehead. The intensity of his dark eyes and those expressive brows. The harsh lines of his nose, cheekbones and profile, softened by his lush mouth and astonishing smile. His five o'clock shadow. His voice. His scent of something citrusy with cedar and the way it makes my blood run hot.

His humor and intelligence. His passion. His mischievous laugh.

His stellar cock.

I shift restlessly in my seat, uncrossing and recrossing my legs as I studiously avoid my father's gaze.

For the record, I've had my share of sex. With Percy

and a couple of other guys during a period when we briefly broke up years ago, when I first arrived in the States for school. Everything from fumbling and awkward teenage sex in the back of some parental car to adequate college sex, quick sex, slow sex, accidental sex and perfectly lovely adult sex. The issue is that I've never had anything approaching Damon sex, which is sex that leaves you as an obliterated and throbbing smudge of creamy lady bits on the floor.

Is it getting warm in here? I adjust the vents until they're aimed directly at my overheated face.

I honestly think he broke something inside me. Because now I have to live with the knowledge that there is a man out there who knows everything about my body already. I don't have to teach him anything or demonstrate anything. He knows it better than I know it myself. And the thought of his knowledge leaves me in a perpetual state of agitated breathlessness. It makes me look for him in every crowd. Strain my ears for the sound of his voice whenever I hear a man speak. Hell, even the thought of his *name* makes my nipples peak and my panties damp.

He's become a bit of an obsession since that night, exactly as I feared he would. That's why I walked out. Well, that and my absolute dread of an awkward morning after. Why not make things easier on both of us and extract myself without forcing him to pretend he wants my phone number? I'm not an expert in one-night stands, but I know *that* much.

I also know that a single interlude with him was enough to provide absolute clarity over my situation with Percy. I have no business connecting with a man the way I connected with Damon and then marrying someone else. *That's* one of the main reasons why I immediately flew back to London and made that final break with Percy. I could never—*ever*—let him touch me again after the way Damon made me feel.

Not that I plan to pin any girlish hopes on a man with whom I shared only a single night. No matter how phenomenal that night was. Especially at this vulnerable transition phase of my life. I don't want or need a man in my life to be happy. I want and need something to do with myself. A career.

"I'm not getting back with Percy, Daddy," I said coldly as the car rolls to a stop in front of a massive and brightly lit brownstone, determined not to foster false hopes in him or anyone else. I gather my clutch and climb out of the car when the driver opens the door for us. I take my father's arm as we head up the steps. "You might as well get used to that idea right now. There's nothing to talk through. I've already said it all."

"Sorry to hear that, poppet," he says out of the corner of his mouth before sliding into his most charming social smile for the benefit of some of our hosts, who stand at the other end of a receiving line in the huge foyer. "Because I invited Percy tonight. Thought it might give you lovebirds the chance to reconnect."

And there in the archway, blonde and handsome in his dark suit and tie, a whiskey in hand and a bright and hopeful smile on his face, stands Percy.

I freeze, my entire face and body slowly turning to concrete around my pleasant smile and my outrage.

"For fuck's sake, Daddy!" I cry out of the side of my mouth. "What did you *do*?"

"You'll thank me later," he says airily.

I proceed, dazed, through endless greetings with

people I don't know in the receiving line, managing what I hope are socially appropriate responses to all the well-wishers.

And then, way too soon, I find myself face to face with my former fiancé.

"I'll leave you to it, Perce," my father says with a hearty shake and a bracing clap on Percy's shoulder. "I did what I could on your behalf, but you've got your work cut out for you tonight."

I do my best to incinerate my father with the strength of my malice, but he seems impervious and zooms away like a rat doggy-paddling away from the *Titanic* while she sinks to the bottom of the Atlantic. Leaving me alone with Percy and the knot of dread lodged deep in my belly.

"Hello, darling," he says.

I privately bristle at the use of the endearment, but I have more pressing concerns as he leans in to kiss me on both cheeks. I pull back as quickly as possible and keep my expression as bland as possible, mindful of any roaming photographers.

"Percy. Didn't expect to see you here tonight."

"I wanted to see you. Plead my case again."

"Percy…"

"You look amazing, by the way." His appreciative gaze sweeps me. "You always do."

"Thanks," I say uncomfortably, determined to extract myself from the situation immediately. "I don't mean to be abrupt, but there's really no point — "

"Is that you, Carly?"

I turn, delighted at the interruption and even more delighted when I see who it is. It's Damon's brother Ryker, smiling and handsome in his dark suit. I can't help but scan the crowd behind him, hoping against hope that Damon is also here tonight, but no such luck. Still, something inside me soars at this renewed connection with Damon and that magical night, no matter how slight. No matter what Damon may or may not have told him about me.

"Ryker." I smile and kiss him on both cheeks, determined to get his last name if nothing else. "Aren't you a handsome devil tonight? So wonderful to see you again."

"You too," he says, turning to Percy with speculative interest as he extends his hand. "Ryker Black. Slight acquaintance of Carly's."

Black! Damon's last name is *Black*, I realize with a delicious flush of pleasure. I could find him again if I wanted to.

Which, I now realize, I desperately do.

"Percy Wilson. Delighted."

"Won't you join us for a drink?" I ask, ridiculously eager to keep Ryker here for as long as possible.

"Love to," he says, a disquieting glimmer of mischief sparking to light in his eyes. "I'll be back in a few. There are some people I need to speak to first."

With that, he strides off into the crowd—still no sign of Damon—and consigns me to more of my private discussion with Percy.

"How do you know him?" Percy asks, a vague note of suspicion in his voice that sets my teeth on edge. In addition to its being none of his business at this point in our relationship, I have no intention of opening a discussion about what may or may not be going on between me and any member of the Black family. "I wasn't aware that you had any connection to the Black family."

"You know them?" I asked, startled.

"Who doesn't? They own half of the city with their real estate empire."

A bell belatedly rings in my brain.

"Hang on. *That* Black family?"

"Of course. Who else?"

I file this fascinating tidbit of information away for later and focus on the issue at hand.

"Percy. I'm sorry, but I have to be honest. I didn't expect to see you here tonight. And as far as I'm concerned, we've already discussed everything we needed to discuss."

"We've been together for years, darling. You don't just scuttle that. We can work things through. No reason why we can't when we haven't told your grandmother or my parents yet."

My grandmother is a touchy issue. I haven't yet told her about the broken engagement. I couldn't face her disappointment on top of everything else when I went home three weeks ago, I suppose. But I can't put it off forever, especially if Percy thinks the fact that I haven't told her yet is a sign that I want to reconcile. Not to mention the fact that if the press gets a whiff that there was an engagement, much less a broken engagement, this whole thing will blow up in my face.

"My grandmother is my problem. I'll tell her soon. But why make me say things to hurt you?" I lower my voice. "I don't love you the way a wife should love her husband. You should be glad to see the back of me."

He tries not to wince but clearly absorbs this the way he would a backhand across the face. Making me feel all the worse.

"I'm not *glad*. I'll never be glad."

"I can't tell you what to do, Percy." I try to hide my

rising impatience and stick to my kind and gentle script as best I can, but I can't stop myself from scanning the crowd for any sign of Damon. Can't help wishing I could swap him out for the man standing in front of me. "But our romantic relationship is over. That's not going to change. We need to work on being friends now."

"I'm not giving up on you," he says.

I can see that.

Feeling suddenly drained and morose, I look away and sip my champagne, wishing I had the power to make Percy move on with his life. And to either permanently eject Damon Black from my thoughts or to make him materialize out of the crowd.

5

DAMON

"DON'T LOSE YOUR SHIT," Ryker says as he emerges from the babbling throng and corners me near the bar, where I have been nursing my second dirty martini and doing my best to avoid all human contact.

I'm entering week four of the nightmare that I've begun to think of as Carly-gate. My exhaustion-fueled mood has worsened every day that I scan the endless New York crowds for that single glorious face that I never find. I'm tired of these episodes of low-key cardiac arrest every time I spy the wrong redhead. I'm furious at myself for the ongoing prideful paralysis that prevents me from trying to track her down and see her again when I *know* I'll never rest until I do.

In short? I'm pissed at her for putting me through this, myself for my inability to get over it, my brother for dragging me to this excruciating event and refusing to allow me to sulk without interruption and the world in general.

I scowl at him accordingly. "The fuck are you talking about? I never lose my shit."

"Your shit's been lost since you met a certain British female. Don't deny it."

My scowl deepens. I confessed the pertinent details about Carly's disappearance during a moment of weakness that I now, obviously, regret.

"Speaking of lost shit, where's your lovely new squeeze Ella? Why isn't *she* here?"

Ryker met said Ella at Bemelmans the same night I met Carly. Let's just say that, from all appearances, Cupid nailed him between the eyes with a particularly big and sharp arrow. This smitten fool can't stop talking about her. He's damn near as out of sorts as *I* am these days.

"She's, ah, not into cocktail parties," he says, his ears turning a satisfying shade of red.

"Too bad." My brothers and I never miss an opportunity to give each other grief. Generally good-natured, but we show no mercy. "Seems like she'd come if she were more into you."

"She's plenty into me. Trust me."

"If you say so."

"And don't try to change the subject. I've got information that's about to change your life."

Sure he does. And my ass shits gold dust and diamonds.

"The clock's ticking on any interest I may have in this conversation," I say, checking my watch.

He smirks at me, never a good sign.

"She's here," he says with a subtle tip of his head toward the far end of the room.

The *she* needs no explanation.

My heart stops. Soaring hope will do that to you when you hardly ever feel it. I forget about my nosy audience of one and nearly give myself whiplash glancing around. And suddenly there it is after weeks of fruitlessly searching for it. Hoping for it. Praying for it.

The fiery auburn hair, pulled back in a sleek ponytail this time. The ivory skin and willowy figure poured into a tight and sexy black suit that bares a healthy amount of cleavage. The patrician profile I feel like I've willed into existence again.

Carly.

I marvel at her beauty and her insistence on presenting this hot librarian look to the world when I've experienced the unleashed tiger that lives inside. I note the tension in her shoulders and tightness in her expression. I hate her for standing there with her drink as though she's a normal person at a normal cocktail reception when she's had my thoughts and my balls in her tight-fisted grasp this whole time.

But I don't hate her nearly as much as I want her.

I freeze while two opposing factions inside me immediately weapon up and go to battle with each other. The proud and angry part insists that I walk over there, grab her by the arm and demand to know what the *hell* she thought she was doing by walking out on me when we both know—or should know—that we're not fucking done with each other. And the humbled and relieved part of me wants me to drop to my knees and thank the God that I don't even believe in for bringing her back across my path. For giving me the opportunity to apologize if I've somehow offended her. For blessing me with another chance to bask in her light and see what she might say or do next.

With any other woman, the angry side would win.

No question. She doesn't want me? No problem. Her loss. The sea is big and full of fish.

But Carly's invaded my head. She's like an octopus that has wrapped her tentacles around my brain, and her tentacles have tentacles. She's been my every waking and sleeping thought for the last three weeks. And I haven't slept. I haven't fucking *slept*.

I register the guy with her for the first time, noting his hungry body language as he leans toward her. My entire body clenches.

"Who's the loser?" I bark.

"He may or may not be her fiancé," my brother tells me.

The fuck he is.

Something raw and primitive gives me a vicious shove between the shoulders, propelling me a step or two toward her with no conscious thought. So much for being proud and aloof. But Ryker clamps a hand on my arm, stopping me.

"What?" I snarl, pulling free. I don't have time for this. What if she slips away again while I'm dealing with this idiot?

"Didn't I just tell you not to lose your shit?" he asks, incredulous.

"Get out of my way or you're going to be scraping this floor clean with your teeth."

Ryker snorts out a laugh that does nothing to improve my mood. "Don't you want to know who she is before you go off half-cocked?"

I keep one eye on her, but she doesn't seem to be going anywhere. And my rabid curiosity gets the best of me, because I still don't even know her last name.

"Who?"

"Her grandmother's the Queen."

"Of?" I say blankly.

"England, you stupid fuck. Her father is Prince Edmund. Duke of Montgomery. She introduced herself as Carly, but her full name is Charlotte Montgomery. *Princess* Charlotte."

My brain reels while he types something on his phone and presses it into my hand.

"Here you go," he tells me. "Take a minute to educate yourself."

I grab the phone, grateful that at least one of us can think clearly.

"You keep eyes on her for me," I say. "It's *your* ass if she walks off before I can talk to her."

"Aye, cap."

I quickly read and scroll with growing astonishment, my adrenaline buzz making my hands unsteady. I catch pictures of her throughout her life, from chubby-cheeked cherub until now. Images of her with her father and with —*oh, shit*—the Queen on the balcony of Buckingham Palace during some big event. Recent snippets about her long-term romance with old Percy over there and speculation about a pending engagement. I also see a recent headline or two about her father's questionable personal financial situation, which may or may not be dire.

I file all of it away for later. When I have time to do more thorough research.

For now? I have everything I need to know.

"Thanks," I say, passing the phone back to my brother.

"We good? I don't want any incidents with you and security tonight."

"We're good," I say, already on my way. I slice my

way through the crowd with surgical precision, scrupu-
lously avoiding eye contact with anyone who may want
to talk to me.

Now is not the time.

I get there fast. Suddenly there she is, standing right
in front of me. Within touching distance, right where I
want her. I can't decide whether I want to wring her
elegant neck for putting me through this turmoil or bear-
hug her into oblivion.

"Excuse me," I say, stepping into her line of sight and
interrupting Percy mid-sentence. "Haven't we met
before?"

Her breath hitches as soon as I begin to speak, her
gaze immediately connecting with mine. I experience a
millisecond's worth of an unguarded reaction from
Princess Carly. Her eyes widen. Her cheeks flood with
color. A hint of a smile curls her lips before she thinks to
stop herself for Percy's benefit. What do these clues add
up to? Unmitigated delight. All of it happens in less than
the time it takes for a hummingbird to flap its wings. But
it's plenty of time for me to learn everything I need to
know. More than enough time for me to both want her a
bit more and hate her a bit more.

If she's this eager to see me again, why the fuck didn't
she stick around and give me half a chance three
weeks ago?

Why did she put me through *this*?

She opens her mouth. Flounders in the face of old
Percy's avid interest.

The pause gives me the chance to savor her anew.
She's got vivid red lips tonight. That slicked-back ponytail. Those things are different. The chemistry crackling
between us is the same.

I snap my fingers. "Kelly, isn't it?"

Her expression sours. "Carly, actually."

There it is. That crisp and chilly accent that makes me want to warm her up again.

"That's right. *Carly*. We met at Bemelmans about three weeks ago. I was there with my brothers. You were waiting for your friend to arrive. I never forget a face. But I never caught your last name."

"Montgomery," she says, doing her best to keep her face neutral but unable to hide the sudden flintiness in her eyes. "And your name is *Ruprecht*, isn't it?"

I laugh. I don't think I'll be able to get one over on her, but that doesn't stop me from trying.

"Close but not quite. It's Damon." I turn to old Percy and extend my hand. "Damon Black. And you are...?"

"Percy Wilson. Pleasure."

I survey my competition, prepared to hate him on sight before quickly deciding that this blue blood is no competition at all. It's right there in his blandly handsome features, double-breasted suit and soft hands. There's no fire here. This guy isn't hungry. He's never sweated over something he wanted or performed a hard day's work like my brothers and I have. He has no true ambitions, probably the result of being to the manor born with a silver pole up his ass. I was also born with a silver spoon, true, but I'm at least ninety percent true ambition. I want to put the Black family empire firmly in the billion-dollar category. By the end of the year. And I will. Mark my words. I achieve my goals or die trying. A man like *this*, on the other hand, could never handle a woman with Carly's spirit—in bed or out.

She may not know that yet. But *I* do.

I almost feel sorry for the man, who clearly suspects

that I want her and that he may well be staring at his replacement in her bed. We're both way out of our league when it comes to a woman like Carly. But *I* have a chance at reaching the inner her. *He* never will.

Satisfied by my assessment, I release his hand and snap my fingers again.

"Hold on," I say, turning back to Carly. "You're Princess Charlotte, aren't you? I saw something about you online recently. Matter of fact, I read something about an engagement. Should I be offering my best wishes?"

They both stiffen, but Carly leaps in to stop the awkward silence before it really takes off.

"You can't believe everything you read online," she says. "I'm surprised you don't know that, Mr. Black."

A worthless non-answer.

"Call me Damon. More than one online rumor has ultimately been confirmed," I say brightly.

"We're not engaged. Not that it's any of your business," she says in arctic tones. *"Mr. Black."*

"If I have *my* way, you'll be offering your best wishes very soon, yes," Percy says with a pointed look in her direction that makes her frown.

"Ah. Sounds like you're more engaged than you thought you were, princess," I say. "Or should I call you *ma'am*? Or would you prefer *your majesty*?"

"Feel free to call me *Ms. Montgomery*, Mr. Black." By this point, it sounds as though she's clipping her syllables with a chainsaw. "Only my grandmother is *her majesty*."

"My mistake, Carly," I say easily, staring her down. That haughtiness really gets under my skin. And to think that people call *me* arrogant. "Looks like I'm just a dumb

American. You're my first princess. I don't know how to behave."

Her nostrils flare. Her face floods with vivid color. For a second, I wonder if she plans to lunge for my throat—a possibility that thrills me somewhat, to be honest—but a new distraction arrives.

"Percy, can I borrow you for a second?" One of tonight's hostesses, a silver-haired woman wearing her body weight in diamonds, appears and puts a hand on Percy's arm, startling the three of us. "My husband is asking about your new polo pony."

"I see." Old Percy divides his speculative and suspicious glance between me and Carly. "Absolutely. Excuse me, darling."

The use of the D-word scrapes my nerves. Renews my anger at Carly.

The hostess and Percy walk off, leaving me alone with Carly and my flaring temper.

I remind myself that we're in the middle of a cocktail reception. Now is not the time for me to lose my shit. But that battle has evidently been lost since the first second I laid eyes on Carly Montgomery here.

I ease closer, taking care to lower my voice.

"Your full of surprises, aren't you, Your Royal Highness?" Ready to pick this fight, I give her a lingering once-over that makes her stiffen. "Where should we start? With your disappearing act, your title or your wannabe fiancé?"

FUMING, I stare into Damon's stony face and gleaming eyes, wondering about my own sanity and trying to decide exactly why I'm so glad to see this arrogant and troublesome prick again. Is the captain of an eighteenth-century merchant vessel glad to see a pirate climb aboard with a cutlass clamped in his teeth? No, he is not. Yet here I am, in all my hormone-drenched foolishness, happy to see Damon again and to realize that he hasn't forgotten me. That maybe our time together meant something to him. Actually, *happy* isn't the word. *Thrilled* is a better choice. *Ecstatic* is probably the best choice. I feel as though an unintended side effect of my walking out of his hotel suite was that he kept control of my ability to breathe and think clearly. Not that I'm thinking clearly now as I take an aggressive step forward and hike up my chin, the better to meet his challenge.

But now, finally, I can *breathe* again.

"Let's start with the fact that I'm *not* engaged. As I believe I just mentioned, had you been paying attention. Not that it's any of your business. And thank you for trying to put me on the hot seat in front of Percy. Charming."

"But you *were* engaged," he says with the shrewdness of a solicitor questioning someone in the witness box.

"Yes," I reluctantly admit.

He hesitates, his gaze hard and searching while he digests this information.

"You cheated on him with me?"

The implication rubs me the wrong way. I resent needing to explain myself to anyone, but the idea that he thinks I'm a cheater—when I grew up witnessing the excruciating implosion of my parents' marriage due to my father's shenanigans—is worse.

"Does it matter?" I snap.

A longer pause this time.

"Yes." His entire body tenses. Even a muscle pulses in his jaw. "Much to my surprise."

Something about the unmistakable turbulence in his expression makes my chest ache.

"We were on a break to evaluate things. If you must know. Now I've ended things."

"You sure about that?"

"Have I become re-engaged without my knowledge?" I frown. "I'm almost positive I haven't."

A glimmer of amusement from Damon. "Old Percy seems confused."

"I can't help that," I say, shrugging.

"Maybe you're sending him mixed messages."

The idea that Damon Black, in all his tall, dark and handsome glory, might be jealous gives me an unreasonable thrill. I'm not proud about it, but there's no denying it.

Still, we're near complete strangers to each other. Boundaries must be set and maintained.

"I'm sorry, but *how* is this any of your business?"

Crooked smile from Damon. "Sweetheart, if you didn't make it my business the first time you smiled at me, it sure as hell became my business when you fucked me."

It's hard to decide what excites me more about him. His crudeness or his possessiveness. It's startling to discover this secret part of me that loves being challenged. And it will be interesting to discover how well matched we are in this battle of wills.

"I wasn't aware that our little interlude together had that sort of significance," I say, knowing it will infuriate him.

Sure enough, his lips pull back in a lopsided grimace that would be right at home on an alligator in the second before it chomped me into oblivion.

"You've been brutally clear on how little it meant to *you*."

The note of hurt in his deep voice catches me off guard. If anything, I'd told myself my disappearing routine would have pinched his ego. It never occurred to me that he may have been upset.

This human side of Damon Black reminds me of one of the reasons why I'm so glad to see him again. He's a very intriguing man. At times like this, there seems to be so much more to him than just his innate sexiness. And uncovering those characteristics seems so much more important than my vow to remain unattached and above the dating fray.

I open my mouth, determined to ask him if we could get a private drink later. To offer an apology. To admit that I may have jumped to conclusions and handled things badly that night.

But my father's voice intrudes before I can get any of that out.

"I didn't know you knew Damon Black, Charlotte," he says, appearing beside us and beaming as though he just got word that my grandmother amended her will to make him the sole heir. His high color and red nose indicate that he's enjoyed another drink or two since our arrival. The knowledge does not thrill me. Nor does his obvious interest in Damon. "Care to make the introductions?"

No, I wouldn't care. Not with that speculative light in my father's eye. Nevertheless, I revert to the crisp manners that have been drummed into me since birth.

"Daddy, this is Damon Black. Real estate magnate. We met briefly at Bemelmans several weeks ago." I pause to shoot Damon a veiled warning look, which he ignores as he shakes my father's hand. "Damon, this is my father, Prince Edmund. Duke of Montgomery."

"Delighted," my father says, pumping his hand.

"Pleased to meet you, sir. I understand that you have quite the personal collection of art."

My father's smile now threatens to swallow his entire head and perhaps eat into his neck. "As do you. I'd love to see your Picasso sketches. I'm sure they're stunning."

As an art lover, I try not to gasp.

"That could be arranged. They're out at my family home on Long Island."

"I look forward to it. And while I have you to myself for the moment, I'd hoped to make some discreet inquiries about selling some of my Baroque pieces."

Damon's interest sharpens. "Really? You'd get the best prices at an auction."

"Yes, but I'd rather do without all the publicity," my father tells him with a rueful grin. "Perhaps we could take a meeting at my home at your convenience? Discuss it further? My private secretary would make all your travel arrangements, of course. And you'd stay at the guest house on the estate."

"I'd like that." Damon's impassive gaze flickers to me, then quickly returns to my father. "I'll take you up on the estate, but I'll just take my jet, thanks."

Jet? He has a *jet*?

"As you wish," my father says.

"I'm free this weekend," Damon says, to my further astonishment. "What about you?"

"I can be," my father says, lighting up like a solar flare.

"Will Carly be there?" Damon smoothly asks my father, his attention flickering to me. "I thought I read something about her being an art history major?"

I freeze, caught somewhere between my desire to be a grown and independent woman who makes her own scheduling decisions, my desire to see Damon again and my fervent wish to have nothing to do with any of my father's financial issues, which may or may not be shady, especially if they grow to somehow involve Damon.

I open my mouth to register a complaint.

"Of course she will," my father booms before I can say anything. "We'll *both* see you very soon. I'll have my private secretary arrange everything."

"Great," Damon says with a *gotcha* gleam in his eye as he turns to me. "I look forward to seeing you both again soon."

With that, he walks off, taking all the air in the room with him and leaving me feeling oddly deflated as I stare after him.

"Did I detect a trace of chemistry between you and our wealthy new friend?" my father asks, a poorly hidden trace of glee in his voice.

"What on earth are you talking about?" I say, as annoyed by the question as I am by the sudden appearance of a gorgeous blonde by Damon's side as he arrives at the bar. It occurs to me that I can't spend the entire evening fighting this irrational jealousy every time some woman blinks in Damon's direction, so I focus on my father. "I barely know the man."

"You'll get to know him. And you could certainly do worse."

"Do worse for *what*?"

"Husband, of course. What else?"

Outrage gets the best of me.

"First of all, I'm not in the market for a husband. Second, you were just advocating for Percy not half an hour ago."

"One rich man's as good as any other," he says, shrugging.

"If you're so determined to solve your financial problems through marriage, allow me to suggest that *you* land a rich wife. And leave me out of it."

"That tone is unnecessary, Charlotte. When you get to be my age, I think you'll find—"

"Sorry, Daddy," I say, spying my chance with Damon when he says something curt to the woman and she turns away, looking disappointed. "Excuse me for just..."

I dash off, intercepting Damon as he accepts a martini from the bartender.

He goes very still at the sight of me. Waits, one brow up.

I stand there like an idiot for several seconds, my courage draining away. It's one thing to plan an articulate and heartfelt apology when I'm safely across the room. Something else again when confronted with the forbidding lines of his tight expression. Not to mention the fact that my royal status makes most people I encounter eager to please. Damon Black evidently hasn't received that memo.

Foolish of me to expect *him* to make this easy for me. *He* is clearly a master of saying whatever the fuck he wants.

I find that wildly exhilarating and refreshing.

"I'm not sure how I feel about this pending visit of yours," I say, bristling under his unforgiving gaze and shelving the apology for now. "Not that you care."

He barks out a humorless laugh. Takes a leisurely sip of his drink.

"And you are a *model* of consideration about other people's feelings, aren't you, princess?"

"Pardon me?"

"You couldn't wake anyone up?" He leans in and lowers his voice, mindful of the crowd that I've already forgotten about. "You couldn't spare two seconds to think about how I'd feel when I woke up and realized you'd split without a word or a note? What happened to the golden rule? They don't teach you basic manners at the palace, princess?"

"Stop calling me that," I snap, undone by his vehemence. "I actually came over to apologize, but maybe this isn't the time. Since you can't be civil."

Damon downs the rest of his drink and slams the empty glass on the bar.

"You're right. I'm pissed off at the world, which is *your* fault. This isn't the time."

And he turns his back on me and walks off *again*, leaving me gaping and foolish at this anticlimactic moment.

For fuck's sake. What am I supposed to do *now*?

"I'm not finished talking to you," I say impotently.

He keeps going without a backward glance.

Well, what's a hormone-crazed girl to do?

I follow him, that's what, hurrying through the crowd with a bland social smile plastered to my face as I track his progress out of the main area and down a long and deserted hallway with several closed doors on either side. I catch up to him as he peers inside the first room, frowns and shuts the door again.

"Damon—"

"Walk away, princess," he says, heading to the next door and checking inside. I catch a glimpse of a dimly lit library. "I'm going to take a piss and then I'm going to leave. I'm trying not to lose my temper with you."

"Well, I've bloody well lost my temper with *you*," I say, hurrying around to block him as he shuts the door, hopefully preventing him from walking off again. "You don't get to dictate the terms of—"

"*I* don't get to dictate?"

The new note in his voice—velvety but also dangerous—catches my attention. So does the unwavering intensity in his eyes.

I know that look. I've been dreaming about that look for three weeks.

The pregnant pause makes my breath catch. My nipples ache.

"*You've* been dictating the terms between us. That stops now," he tells me.

I shake my head, wild excitement coursing through me.

"Stop looking at me like tha—"

He laughs.

Laughs.

There's no further warning before he grabs my wrist with one hand, opens the door again with the other hand and pulls me into the library before slamming the door shut with his foot.

7

CARLY

MY ASTONISHMENT quickly gives way to a dizzying wave of relief. Yes, *relief*. Relief to have found him again when I was so afraid he was gone forever. To touch him again. Most of all? Relief that he has snatched the reins from my hands and is firmly in control of this thing that we both seem to want and need.

I drop my clutch. We come together in a kiss that feels hard and punishing but also gloriously welcome. He makes a masculine sound of triumph as he grabs my ponytail and uses it to angle my head back for better access to my mouth. I open for his tongue as it slips inside, desperate to take him deeper. To drown in his sophisticated scent of incense and amber. My arms and hands move on their own, eagerly wrapping around his shoulders and seeking the solidity of his scalp beneath that thick hair. I press my body tight against his. Tighter. And when that is still not close enough, I wrap a leg around his thigh. My reward for this bold move in the middle of a cocktail reception that includes my father? Damon's groan of encouragement as he plants his hands on my ass, lifts me so I can wrap both legs around his waist and tumbles me down to the nearest leather sofa.

He stretches out on top of me and settles there—ah, God, right *there*—in the cradle between my hips, his unyielding cock unerringly hitting my sweet spot with every powerful thrust as he finds the perfect rhythm. I cry out, unable to keep the spiraling jolts of gathering ecstasy inside my body.

"Quiet down, little tiger," he says in that black-velvet voice as he locks his hips in place. "If you think I'm going to let you come before you apologize, you'd better think again."

"I'm sorry." The words, bottled up inside since almost the moment the door to his hotel suite clicked shut behind me, can't pour out of my mouth fast enough. It's a relief to confess. To own it. "I'm so *sorry.*"

"For…?"

"For walking out on you like that."

"Why did you?"

I teeter on the edge of a shattering orgasm as I struggle to catch my breath and get my words right.

"I was afraid it would be awkward in the morning. Or that you'd kick me out when you woke up."

A humorless laugh from Damon. *"Kick you out?* Your situational awareness needs serious work."

"I know," I whisper. "I'm so stupid."

"You're not stupid. But don't pull a fucking stunt like that again."

"I won't." I palm his face and pull him in again because I've had enough talking. "I *won't.*"

"Did you think about me?"

"Constantly. It's been very annoying."

The hint of his smile gives way to another sumptuous

kiss. More uncontrollable cries from me as he grips my ass to anchor me and his hips began to swivel. The gleam of dark amusement in his eyes as he watches me helplessly unravel.

"Does he touch you like this? Make you crazy like this? *Percy?*"

I laugh. The question is so absurd. "You *know* he doesn't. You think this is normal behavior for me? Any of it?"

The flash of that pirate's smile from Damon.

"You were going to marry *him*? Anyone can see you'd be bored to tears. You'd make mincemeat out of him by dinner. That's plain as the nose on my face, and I've only known you for ten minutes."

"Yes, well, where were you when I was telling him *yes*?"

"I'm here now. And no one else touches you."

He may have me where he wants me and I may well have overdosed on his pheromones, but I still resist being told what to do.

"*I'll* decide who touches me and who doesn't," I say.

"It's not up for discussion."

He's right. It's not. Not when he slowly trails his fingers across the top of my bosom, right at the lacy edge of my camisole, at the same time as a particularly well-placed thrust.

I fly apart, raw pleasure making my heart stop, my back arch and entire body stiffen. He holds me while I ride it out, until the last aftershocks ripple through my cooling body, leaving only embarrassment and growing uncertainty.

Oh my God.

What did I just do?

What did I just *say*?

I push his shoulders to get him to release me, which he does reluctantly before standing and turning away to adjust his trousers. His face is shadowed, his expression indecipherable. I scramble up to sitting, the better to examine the enormity of what just happened.

My sleek ponytail is now a mess. I'm sure that we're both wearing my bright red lipstick all over our lower faces, although the dim lighting hides the full scale of *that* disaster. My panties are wet, my nipples hard. His jacket does little to hide the bulge between his legs. We're in the middle of a cocktail reception *with my father present*.

Worst of all?

I have no idea where Damon and I stand, although I seem to have just unabashedly thrown myself at him.

And I can't swear that I won't do it again as soon as the opportunity presents itself.

We regard each other warily until the silence becomes too much for me and I say the first thing that pops into my mind.

A nasty habit of mine, I admit.

"I assume you're trying to humiliate me by making your point," I say, trying to smooth my hair, quickly giving up in the absence of a magic wand and looking around for my clutch. "Well done."

He scowls. "Again. Situational awareness. I'd never try to humiliate you. I'm reminding you."

"Of?"

He doesn't seem to care for my snotty attitude. Or maybe it's the scathing look I shoot him as I stand up and head for my clutch over on the floor. Whatever.

He grabs my wrist for the second time tonight,

ignores my gasp of surprise and flattens my hand over his cock. Which is still rock hard and straining for me.

"I'm into you." He plants both his hands over mine, guiding me into a rough caress that I eagerly mimic. Clearly, it doesn't take much to make me follow where he leads. "I'm not thrilled about it. I tried to pretend that I'm not. That's why I didn't try to track you down when it would have been easy to hire an investigator to find you."

I frown. An *investigator*?

"What are you talking about?"

"I'm talking about my pride. When you walked out? I said, *Fuck her*. I'm not chasing anyone. I'm not playing games."

"Oh," I say, disappointment and dread trickling through me. Unfortunately, I'm not a good enough actress to hide my reaction. Hell, I'm a mess. A recently broken engagement. No career to speak of. Sending mixed messages to Damon. What thinking man with half a brain would want anything to do with me in my current state? "I see."

"Don't worry." Self-deprecating smile from Damon. "I changed my mind. If we can be together like *this*?" He thrusts against my hand, making renewed desire coil low in my belly. "Fuck pride."

I stare at this man, riveted by his sexiness and his vulnerability. By his occasional openness and by all the secrets hidden behind those dark eyes. I remind myself that I'm not in the market for anything, and, even if I were, this would not be the man on which to hang relationship hopes. He could slay me with little effort on his part.

Absolutely *slay* me.

"What now?" I ask.

"Now I want you to get the hell out of here and think about how hard I am for you. How hard I've been every fucking night because you want to play games and seem to get off on making me crazy with your knee-jerk reactions."

"I don't—"

"Yeah. You do. So take a minute and picture me trying to fall asleep like *this*. Do you touch yourself in the shower? Next time, think about how much I wish I were there, licking the water off your breasts."

I gape at him, the seething erotic images making speech impossible.

"Think it over. *I* think we should spend some time together. Get to know each other. See what happens. Let me know if you're up for that."

We stare at each other, the silence mushrooming as I think about all the ways and times we could fuck each other if I only said the word.

Honest to God, I can't think when he looks at me like that.

"That's it?"

"That's it." He blows out a breath and roughly rubs his hands over the top of his head, ruffling his hair. "Actually, hang on. Give me your phone."

I slowly continue my trajectory, retrieve my clutch from the floor and return to hand him my phone. Then I watch him input his information, my stomach turning with a strange combination of anxiety and jubilation the entire time. There's got to be a catch here somewhere. I'm just not clever enough to spot it. A smart, exciting and sexy guy like Damon Black can't just be a smart, exciting and sexy guy. There must be a troll, pedophile or, hell, serial murderer hidden in there somewhere. Or, if he *is* as smart, exciting and sexy as he seems, his arrogant streak probably reaches titanic proportions and/or he's already married three times and has mistresses stashed in every major city in the world.

My life just doesn't suddenly get this exciting and easy.

"Here." He hands me back my phone with grim satisfaction. "Call me when you're ready to explore this thing."

I numbly glance at my phone, then zero in on him again. "So that's it. I call you whenever I'm ready."

"Fuck no." He looks at me as though I've taken the decision to become a professional sumo wrestler. "You've got forty-eight hours to get reasonably ready. After that, I'm hiring those investigators and showing up on your doorstep. Bye."

I laugh shakily. "I don't know whether to ask you to come home with me or slap your face."

"Figure it out. Bye. No, wait. Come here."

I eagerly walk back into the danger zone of the magnetic field surrounding his body, my foolish head full of wild ideas about how we could lock the door and return to the sofa for a round two. So it's with some disappointment that I watch Damon extract a handkerchief from his breast pocket and use it to wipe my mouth before wiping his own. I linger when he's done, a hopeful light no doubt shining in my eyes.

"No more kisses for you tonight." He gives me an X-rated once-over that does little to cool my overheated blood. "I'm cutting you off until you do the right thing."

I can't stifle a bark of surprised laughter. "You're a *horrible* man. You know that?"

"Then why do you want me so much, princess?" he asks silkily.

"No idea."

I walk out, propelled by the galling sound of his knowing laughter behind me. The lively sound of the cocktail reception in full swing returns in a rush. Luckily, the hallway is still deserted, so there's no one to see me turn in a flustered circle while I try to decide which door is likeliest to lead to the washroom. The second try is the charm. I lock the door and flip on the light, braced for the worst as I face the mirror.

Aaand it's worse than that.

I set my phone on the counter and attack my hair first, digging in my clutch for my tiny comb and making liberal use of the luxury beauty products laid out for the guests. My lipstick-smeared mouth, which looks as though it's been used to test makeup for the next *Joker* movie, takes longer.

As for my feverish color, bright eyes and fumbling hands?

Nothing I can do.

"Get a grip, Charlotte," I tell my reflection, rubbing my chest to slow my heartbeat. From there? Easy enough to flatten my palms and run them over my nipples in a fruitless attempt to stop the aching. To wish Damon's hands were touching me instead.

Damon freaking Black.

I'm a mess and it's all his fault. Worse, I can't stand this uncertain purgatory of not knowing when I'll see or speak to him again. It was hard enough to walk out of the library just now.

Another wild impulse—I'm just full of them these

days—makes me call him, excitement keeping me in a stranglehold while the phone rings.

"Hello?"

I take a deep breath. "Charlotte Montgomery calling," I say in my crisp phone voice. "May I speak with Damon Black, please?"

I literally hear him smile. This, naturally, makes me smile.

"Speaking."

"You've made an absolute disaster of my hair and makeup. I thought you should know."

"I regret nothing."

"Smug bastard. Now I'm not sorry for leaving you in that state. How are your privates, by the way?"

"Still blue. The sound of your voice in my ear doesn't help."

I grin at myself, ridiculously pleased. "Do take care of things down there. It's an exceptionally fine cock."

"Glad you feel that way," he says, his voice husky now.

I turn away from the mirror and lean against the counter, balancing the phone against my shoulder.

"Speaking of my new favorite subject," I say softly, "I find it ironic that, according to you, I'm supposed to remain untouched. Yet your cock is free to do whatever it bloody well pleases. How is that fair?"

He also lowers his voice until it becomes a soft and seductive murmur. "You'll be happy to know that my dick is only interested in *you*. Which has been a wildly annoying and inconvenient development recently. So you have nothing to worry about."

"That *is* good news," I say, caught off guard by a sudden wave of wistfulness. "I missed you, you know."

Long and serrated breath from Damon.

"I missed *you*."

There's a pause, during which I try to resist the knowledge that he's right here in the building with me, just a couple of doors down. But it seems prudent to slow down this runaway train. No matter how much I don't want to.

"So how will we handle this, Damon? Shall I Google you? Find out everything, including your pet hamster's name when you were in primary school?"

"Let's do it the old-fashioned way. Ask each other questions. Listen to the answers. Learn about each other."

Unfortunately, the number one question that needs answering has to do with when I'll see him again.

"Yes, well, the main thing you need to know about me is that I eat dinner every single night," I say. "And I get hangry when I'm not fed."

I wait, breath held.

"I'll see you tomorrow at eight. Sharp. Wear your hair down."

"Cheeky bastard."

8

DAMON

"WHAT ON EARTH do you think you're doing?"

The blast of Carly's irritated voice from her intercom the following night makes me laugh as I stand outside on her stoop.

"Feeding you as promised," I say, carefully balancing my grocery bags. I'm pleased to confirm that—as I'd expected—her building seems solid and safe. Inside, a security guard watches me with some amusement from his post behind a marble desk. I'm not sure why my dumb ass seems to suddenly think I'm personally responsible for this woman's well-being, but there's no shaking the feelings of protectiveness and satisfaction. "I can't feed you by eight if I don't get started early. Are you going to let me up?"

"You're forty-five minutes early," she says, her tone now suggesting that she's going to use her sharpest chef's knife to divest me of my balls the second I set foot in her apartment. "And I was promised a fancy restaurant."

"No, you weren't. If anything, I promised you a delicious meal. Which I will provide. But I want privacy and your undivided attention."

"That's all well and good, but I've just got out of the shower. I haven't done hair or makeup. I look like the hag from all the Grimm brothers' fairytales."

"Doubtful. Buzz me in. I'm not here to see how good you are with hair and makeup. I want to see you in your natural state in your natural habitat."

"Be careful what you wish for, you foolish man," she mutters darkly as the door unlocks.

I emerge from the elevator a couple minutes later to find her waiting for me down at the end of a long and elegant hallway, her *you're dead* glower firmly in place as I approach. She's wearing a tank top and running shorts, a combo that wins my wholehearted approval because it shows the long stretch of her shapely legs and the intriguing straps of a pink bra across her pale shoulders. On her head? A white towel wrapped tight. And her flashing light-colored eyes are now, *finally*, brightly lit enough for me to detect their color.

"*Blue*," I say softly, mesmerized as I stare down at her fresh face, which features a sun-kissed sprinkling across her nose. "With freckles."

"Well done," she says, a smile reluctantly trying to break through. "You've demonstrated your proficiency with primary colors *and* solved a pressing mystery."

"Everything about you is a pressing mystery, princess. But you don't listen very well, do you? What'd I tell you about your hair?"

"You're far too demanding and far too interested in my hair. I'm tempted to shave it all off just to smite you. Nip your fetish in the bud."

I shrug easily. "Everything about you is a fetish. Tick-tock."

She rolls her eyes. Blushes furiously. And removes the towel to reveal wet spirals of fiery hair that tumble across her shoulders and frame her head in a glorious halo.

"Anything else before I let you in? Any other ridiculous demands?" she asks.

"Yeah. Start getting your head around the fact that you're gorgeous. Just like that. Anything else is putting a cherry on top of a flawless diamond."

Her breath hitches. "Are you trying to turn my head?"

"Hate to tell you, but we've already given each other whiplash. At this point, we don't need to impress each other. We need to get to know each other."

If I've told a bigger lie in the last ten years, I can't think of it. Not the part about getting to know each other. That's a thousand percent true. So is the part about *her* not needing to impress *me*. But *me* not needing to impress *her*?

Big-ass lie.

I'm all about impressing her. Hence the cooking tonight. I want to show her my real estate holdings, my investment portfolio and my bank account balances. I can't wait to show off my various luxury cars and the jet. Don't get me started on my penthouse with its 360-degree views that include the rivers or our family home in the Hamptons.

I want her to see all of it. To understand that I plan to hit the billionaire mark—both with the company and personally—or die trying.. To know that I can afford and protect a woman like *her*.

And none of it has to do with the fact that she's a royal.

When I get a minute, I'm going to think about how ironic it is that I'm positive both that Percy could never be the man for her and that I am the man for her, yet equally positive that she will wise up to me and/or I will blow it if given half the chance.

Can I pedal hard and put a good face on it? Yeah, sure.

But the bottom line, independent of my financial bottom line, is that I'm a worthless loser who drives people away no matter how hard I work to keep them. My mother walked out on me. Carly has already walked out on me once. The clock is ticking on when she does it again.

My only job? To impress her enough to make her think twice before she does it.

"Can I come in?" I ask.

She stands aside with a flourish, ushering me inside a great apartment with plenty of light and space. Gourmet kitchen. The works. Exactly what you'd expect, even if it does seem like a lot for one person. But my own apartment is huge, so I can't talk.

"Nice," I say, then set my things on the counter and wash my hands before diving into the bags. "I'm making pasta with vodka sauce and salad in case you're vegetarian. I can add meatballs if you're not. If you're vegan, you're making your own damn dinner. You're in charge of the salad. I assume you can chop without losing fingers."

She grabs a knife and a cutting board, brows raised. "I'll have you know I'm an excellent cook."

"Yeah?" I eyeball her with new respect. "How'd that happen?"

"Mum wanted to make sure I had one foot in the regular world. She wanted me to be a normal kid who knew what to do without a nanny or a housekeeper fussing over me. I've always cooked, cleaned and done my own laundry. My father was baffled by the whole thing, but there you have it." Her expression turns wistful. "She had the common sense in the family. I miss her."

I pause, riveted by any detail about her personal life and determined to show her that she can trust me. "When did she die?"

"Couple of years ago. She and Daddy had a terrible divorce that lasted roughly as long as the marriage. In case you're interested."

"I *am* interested." I pass her the veggies and choose my words carefully, surprised that I'm willing to share these shameful details from my past with anyone, much less share them this early in the relationship. "I know about nasty divorces. My mother walked out when I was ten. When my father went through some financial difficulties and almost lost everything." I clear my throat, my voice turning husky. "Married my father's richer best friend. They had a custody war. Then she, ah, died in a car accident before we ever really reconciled."

"I'm sorry to hear that," she says softly. "And your dad?"

Shaky laugh from me. "I'm supposed to be cooking dinner. Not sure why I'm getting into all this with you."

She regards me with steady warmth, as though she knows exactly how hard this is. "It's because I'm an incredibly special person. Anyone can see that."

I sure as fuck can.

"My dad never quite recovered from her walking out. He rebuilt the companies to some extent. Brought me and my brothers in once we got out of school. And then got lung cancer and died before we took things to the next level. Never got to see what my brothers and I could do."

Sad nod from Carly. "Very inconsiderate of him."

I snort. "We thought so."

Another nod as she takes her time about choosing her words. "Thank you for telling me."

"Yeah, well," I say gruffly, looking around for a pot, "if you give me half a chance to ruin the evening, I'm going to take it."

The bright burst of her laughter breaks up the mood as she finds the pot for me and passes it over.

"This date sucks, to be honest. No hair and makeup. No fancy dinner out. I didn't even get a hello kiss. We should give some thought to calling the whole thing off. You're a terrible disappointment."

With that, she turns to a new cabinet and reaches for wineglasses, giving me a stellar view of her toned ass and thighs as she reaches.

I grab my chance. Like Lin-Manuel Miranda says, I'm not throwing away my shot.

Coming up behind her, I lean against her warm body and wrap her up tight, pressing one of my hands on her torso, my thumb resting in the valley between her breasts, and the other low on her belly, my fingertips just grazing her pussy. She shudders and melts into me, exactly the way I'd hoped she would. At this close range, her scent acts as a hyper-charged aphrodisiac, demanding that I press my nose to her curls and try to identify it. There's a hint of berries. Of lavender. Of something indefinable that's entirely *her*.

Since she wants her kiss, I nudge aside enough hair to reach her bare skin and nuzzle my way to where the tender curve of her neck meets her shoulder. I latch on to that sensitive point, licking and nuzzling just enough to make her shiver and coo.

"You've *got* to stop touching me," she says helplessly. "I can't fucking *think* when you do."

There's only one sensible response to that.

"Then don't think."

I tighten my grip. Revel in this moment, which I consider to be my reward for focusing hard and working my ass off all day to close my latest deal. And I remind myself that we're getting to know each other tonight, so now is not the time for me to bend her over the counter and take her from behind. Much as I desperately want to. The last thing I want to do is leave her with the impression that all I want is a quick fuck.

This right here? With her?

It's *more*. It's special. It deserves my best shot. Even if it leaves me with a terminal case of blue balls.

"I lived for that," I say, reluctantly letting her go and backing up a step. "All day."

She turns to face me, her color high and her eyes feverishly bright. And I'd hardly be a heterosexual man if I didn't notice the way her breasts heave as she tries to catch her breath and the prominent dots of her nipples through her thin bra and top.

But it's the unmistakable uncertainty behind her searching look that really catches my attention.

"What're we playing at here, Damon?"

Good question. I can only shrug and wish I knew, because this thing between us? Scary as hell.

"I was hoping you'd tell me," I say.

"My life is already complicated. I'm trying to figure out my life and my career. I've got a recent broken engagement under my belt and an overbearing father breathing down my neck." She hesitates, that hint of vulnerability intensifying in her expression. "I'm trying to be open with you. The last thing I need is anything emotional. Or any, I don't know, *confusion*. Am I making any sense?"

I feel another surge of something primitive and protective. Maybe it's because it's just the two of us here in her apartment and she's giving me a glimpse of the fresh-faced young woman beneath the Titian goddess who strode into Bemelmans and slid under my skin. Maybe it's because I know, even at this ridiculously early stage of things, that I will kill or die before I allow this woman to be hurt on my watch. And make no mistake, my watch began pretty much the second I met her.

As long as she continues to look at me like *that*? We're golden.

"You're making perfect sense," I tell her.

"So…we're keeping it casual?"

I frown. The C-word scrapes over my nerves, which is weird because I'm all about casual. Any other time, *I'm* the one raising the C-word at the beginning of any interaction with a new woman. Hell, if I could make women sign a release stating they understand the casual nature of our relationship and promising to never mention, say, holidays, meeting relatives and/or marriage, I would.

"It is what it is," I say. "We're figuring out what it is. Why label it?"

"Like I just said. I don't want to get confused or…"

She trails off, leaving a ghostly imprint of the word she didn't say.

Hurt. She doesn't want to get *hurt*.

Well, neither the fuck do I.

"The only thing you need to be clear on at this stage is that you're not marrying Percy." I realize that I don't want to see her reaction to this pronouncement and hastily turn away, my face burning. Normally, if a gorgeous woman wants to hop into bed with me, I don't ask questions. As long as I've got a string of condoms and her husband/boyfriend/girlfriend/significant other isn't using the butt of a pistol to pound on the bedroom door, I've got no problems. Her personal life is none of my business. I'm too busy empire-building to give a fuck. Too busy trying to cross that billion-dollar mark. Which is another indication of how different and scary this thing with Carly is. Matter of fact, this entire conversation is threatening to give me hives, so I grab the pot and head to the sink to fill it. "That, and make sure you don't cut yourself while you're working on the salad. I'm not planning on making a run to the emergency room tonight."

I brace myself for stinging comeback, but there's a welcome interruption in the form of my vibrating phone.

"Sorry," I tell her as I pull it out of my pocket, my ears still hot. "This is Griffin. We're working on a huge deal. I need to talk to him before he heads into a conference call with Tokyo."

"Of course," she says, looking flustered. "I'm running to the loo anyway. I'll leave you to it."

I wonder what the hell I'm getting myself into here as I watch her hurry off—I'm betting she feels as grateful for the reprieve as I do—then hit the button.

"Yeah," I say.

"Trouble in paradise," my brother says. "I'm hearing rumors that their funding will be an issue."

"Shit."

"I'll keep you posted. I'll have a chance to call again during the break."

"So what are our chances of this thing going through?" I say, experiencing a tension spike through my shoulders. Without Tokyo, my billion-dollar dreams are shot, for this year at least. Not the end of civilized society as we know it, but maybe my ambitions wouldn't burn so bright and I could turn down the volume on the *fucking loser* soundtrack always playing in the back of my mind. "Fifty-fifty?"

"Eh, probably better than that. Keep a positive thought. Gotta go."

"Fuck," I say, hanging up and putting the phone away just as Carly reappears in the kitchen doorway.

"Oh no," she says with an exaggerated frown. "You're looking very grumbly now. What's happened? Do I need to take your phone away while you cook dinner? I don't want to be forced to eat overcooked and under-seasoned pasta."

Just like that, she shifts my mood again. One of the reasons she's such a joy to have around.

"We're trying to close on a huge deal in Tokyo. There's a funding issue. Makes life messy."

Her attention sharpens. "Yes, you're a real estate magnate, I believe?"

I laugh. "Yep. That's what I put on my tax returns. That or *Real Estate Emperor*."

"Now I don't feel so bad," she says, grinning as she picks up her knife and begins to chop. "Guess what I have to put on my forms when someone asks my profession?"

"What?"

"Princess of the United Kingdom."

I grimace. "That's horrifying."

"I know! So what's this building, then? It must be particularly important, judging by the look on your face when I walked in. Center for curing cancer? Ground zero for the war on climate change?"

I stifle a snort of laughter. "Real estate is not a laughing matter. Kindly give me the absolute respect and deference that I deserve. High-rise apartments. What else?"

"Sounds fancy," she says, showing impressive skills with her knife. "Did you always want to be in real estate? Growing up?"

I think that over. "Did I always want to pull together funding and structure these complicated deals? No. Did I want to work with my father to rebuild his company and make him proud of me? Yes."

"Well, I certainly understand making parental figures proud," she mutters, pursing her lips. "Trying to, anyway."

"Yeah?" By now I've progressed to seasoning the chicken, but I pause, intrigued. "Is there a story there?"

"Course. But we are talking about *your* story right now. Stop trying to distract me. So you're happy being a real estate emperor?"

I have a tough time coming up with an answer to this baffling question.

"The Black family is in real estate. My name is Damon *Black*, which means that *I'm* in real estate. What's the puzzle?"

"Yes, but are you fulfilled?" she says, sounding bemused.

I open my mouth but, again, no answer is immediately forthcoming.

"I'm a force to be reckoned with. I get to buy the toys I want when I want them. That's fulfilling."

"So that's what you want in life? Toys and respect?"

"No," I say before I think to stop myself. "I want to *win*. I want my holdings to have nine zeros before the decimal point. Which should happen this year if I stay on track and this sale doesn't fall through."

As a generally smart guy who's fended off more than his fair share of gold diggers and Mrs. Damon Black wannabes, I really should know better. You don't shoot off at the mouth about your net worth and then hope people want you for you. Not a strategic move.

On the other hand, there's something so disarming about Carly that I can't seem to fend her off. It's like she sneaks inside my brain and steals these little secrets before I can stop her. And I'm still fighting this overwhelming urge to prove to her that I'm worth keeping around for a while.

Is it twisted for her to want me for me while also wanting her to give me credit for being a baby billionaire?

Yes.

Does Carly have my thoughts twisted into abnormal positions?

Also yes.

Do I care?

Evidently not.

Does my relentless desire to win at everything and

have the most money have anything to do with my mother leaving my father for his richer best friend?

What do I look like? A shrink?

I freeze, knowing I've said too much as I await her judgment.

"You sound like me, you know," she says, a shadow crossing her expression. "The part about doing what you're doing because it's what your family does. Not because it's what you decided to do or wanted to do. Just because it's always been that way, so why not? Only…is that the right way? Doing it so you won't rock the boat?"

I get the feeling she's asking herself as much as me.

"Isn't it? Is there some other way?"

"I hope so," she says thoughtfully. "Because I'm not marrying Percy because my family want me to or expect it. I've got to put my big-girl knickers on and tell my grandmother I've ended the engagement. And that I don't want to serve as patron for every bloody boring charity committee just because someone higher on the food chain can't be bothered. That's not what I want for my life."

"What do *you* want for your life?" I ask, the sudden urgency my voice catching me by surprise.

"I don't want to be stuck in the English countryside. I want to stay here. I love New York."

"Works for me," I say with quiet triumph. "What else?"

"I'm afraid to say it aloud," she says with a rueful laugh. "My father thinks it's a crazy idea."

"What?"

"I'm a painter. I'd love to sell my work. See if I can make a living with that somehow."

"Are you any good?"

She hesitates. I get the feeling that her innate humility or lack of confidence slows her down, but then, much to my pleasure, she takes a deep breath and nods.

"I'm excellent."

"Then why would that be a crazy idea, princess?"

She lights up, blossoming like a June rose right in front of my eyes. A smile like that feels like a tiny taste of winning the lottery.

"You know something about art, right? I'd love to show you some of my work in the spare bedroom later. I use it for a little studio."

"I'd love to," I say.

"Good." Her smile widens until she glows. *Glows.* And if someone snuck in, tapped me on the shoulder and asked what I wouldn't do to keep seeing that exact smile, I'd say a clear and heartfelt *nothing.* "Any idea what *you* want for *your* life?"

You, whispers something inside me. *I want* you, *Carly.*

I swallow the words back with difficulty. They don't seem to want to stay in my mouth. It takes me longer to manufacture a socially acceptable answer.

"I'll have to give that some thought."

"I think you should," she says seriously. "Assuming that building apartments in Tokyo isn't the only thing you can think of for fulfillment. What about charity work? Do you have a foundation?"

"We have the literacy foundation that my father started."

"So you're passionate about that?"

"About people learning to read? Let's call that a *yes,*" I say.

"I'm going to chuck this bar towel right at your smug

face if you don't start giving me serious answers," she says, taking aim. "How would you like *that*?"

I laugh again. Swear to God, I've laughed more in the last ten minutes with her than I have in the last six months.

"Right now, I'm serious about getting dinner on the table before eight. I don't want to risk you getting hangry on me."

"Fair point," she says, slinging the towel over her shoulder. "You get to work."

I produce a stellar pasta dinner, which she eats with gusto. None of that pushing the food around on her plate bullshit I've encountered when dating models. She finishes the dishes like a champ, further confirming that she's no princess when it comes to housework. After that, we settle on the sofa with the last of our wine. That's when I notice the spread on her coffee table. Mystery books by Mary Higgins Clark and—

"What's with all the cat info here?" I say, studying a page printed from some animal shelter website.

"I'm thinking about getting a cat," she says happily. "I love having my own space, but it gets a bit lonely, doesn't it? I think a cat might be good company. Do you like cats?"

"Cats are cool."

She shuffles through the papers and produces a picture that looks like a dust mop with eyes. "How about this one? Her description says she likes to snuggle."

"I'm guessing she also likes to shed."

"You're right," she says, frowning as she tosses the paper back on the table. "I hadn't thought of that. This whole cat business is all very complicated."

"You'll figure it out," I say, surrendering to the temptation to touch her and smoothing her hair behind her ear.

"I feel so unsettled in my life," she says quietly. "It was always the plan for my roommates to move out after graduation. But now it feels like there's too much space. Not enough company. And it's not that I don't like to be alone with my thoughts. It's just... I don't know. I'm blathering. You probably don't get lonely, do you?"

And there goes another one of her complicated questions, detonating over my head like a missile strike.

On any other day, if anyone else had asked me if I felt lonely, the answer would be simple. *Fuck no.* I'm too busy building my empire to be lonely. I careen from meeting to meeting, phone call to phone call, country to country. I'm surrounded by people. I'm sick of people. A lot of the time, my fondest wish is to shipwreck myself on an island in the South Pacific with only a bottle of tequila and my e-reader to keep me company while I devour espionage thrillers. As for female companionship? An hour in bed a few times a week to address our bodies' needs and to help me blow off steam is good, thanks. No need to linger, and don't let the door hit you on the ass on your way out.

But this isn't any other day. This is *Carly* asking. And she's nailing me with her vivid blue x-ray vision while she's at it.

I think about all the meals I eat alone. All the times I walk into my empty apartment after a long day or a grueling trip and there's no one there to be happy I'm back or even to have noticed that I was gone. Which is *every* time I walk into my apartment. I go to bed and wake up by myself. I'm always the unmatched singleton at dinner parties. I managed a personal best time at the

New York Marathon last fall, the third time I'd run the race, and there were plenty of people to grab breakfast with after. But no one to give me a hug and kiss and say, *I'm so proud of you, honey*. No one to fuss over my aching muscles and give me a massage. I'm already in training for this fall's marathon. I pound out all those miles alone.

Alone. Alone. *Alone*.

I open my mouth because Carly is starting to look at me funny. Out shoots the real answer, and it's a doozy. One I probably would never have recognized, much less admitted, until she asked me.

"I get lonely, yeah."

She nods, looking reassured that she's not the only one. "I don't know about you, but I'm taking drastic action to nip this self-pitying *lonely* nonsense in the bud," she says crisply. "Hence the cat. I'm also thinking about volunteering at the cat shelter, because I really love cats. I like to stay busy."

"Me too."

"Also, I'm thinking about joining a running group," she says, pointing to a pair of battered running shoes parked under a console in the hall. "I'm quite good, actually. I've run several short races, but I'm thinking that with some training I could work up to the city marathon next— Why are you looking at me like that? Have I got pasta stuck in my teeth and you didn't tell me?"

I stare at her, frozen inside my astonishment, and desperately try to get a grip. *She's* lonely. *I'm* lonely. *She* likes to run. *I* like to run. Big freaking deal. It's not like I just discovered that she's the reincarnated soul of Juliet and I'm Romeo. No star-crossed lover bullshit here.

But, I gotta tell you, all these little things about her

are starting to add up to something that feels pretty fucking significant.

"I, ah…" Sudden hoarseness forces me to clear my throat. My fidgety hands need something to do, so I rub my thighs a couple of times. "No, I just need to, ah, head home."

Her expression falls until she looks like a kid watching the Grinch steal every single present under the tree on Christmas Eve. Then, in a flash, she locks it all away where I can't see it and presents me with the aloof façade she wore when she walked into Bemelmans and into my life.

"Of course." Cool smile that never touches her eyes as she stands. "I'd thought that we might watch a movie, but you probably wouldn't want—"

"*Don't,*" I say, taking her hand and squeezing it because I can't keep my feelings to myself any better than I can stand to witness the veiled hurt on her face. I stare up at her, eager for her to see my sincerity. "I want. You *know* I want. I've got a shit-ton of emails to get through and calls to make tonight, and I would love to set up a workstation on your dining room table just so I could watch you watch TV while I do it. But I'm not sure you know what you want when it comes to me. I'm only here to give you a taste of the way things could be if you figure it out. I'm not playing games here. This is not a game to me. So think about that."

She nods, her expression shadowed. Then, as though she can't help herself, she pulls her hand free and cups my head on both sides, scratching my scalp with her short nails as she grips my hair and pulls me close enough to hug. Close enough for me to press my face between her breasts and absorb her scent.

But this taste of Carly is more than I can take. Like I said, I'm not playing games. And she's already got me teetering on the edge of my self-control.

So I give myself one second—one short second—to nuzzle her breasts and squeeze her hips before I push her away and stand beside her.

"I may have to go to Tokyo," I tell her, my voice husky.

She nods, two blazing patches of color concentrated in her cheeks. "Okay."

"I'll see you in London this weekend. At your father's."

"Okay."

"Doesn't your grandmother live in London?"

"She does," she says with a startled laugh.

I nod with grim satisfaction. "Good. I hope you get your shit together this weekend. With her and with Percy, just in case you two have any lingering loose ends to tie off. Because I'm not sharing you."

This, naturally, makes her bristle. She straightens her spine.

"I'm not a bag of crisps to be shared or not shared. If I want to respond to Percy when he texts me, I'll do that. I'm allowed to be friends with him if I choose to and if he wants it."

I feel a humorless smile tug on one corner of my mouth. This woman is so smart, sexy and beautiful. So intriguing. So maddening.

"I'm not arguing," I say flatly. "I'm not getting into semantics. Whatever the fuck you are? You belong with *me*. And we both know it. So get your shit together. This weekend."

"I DO HOPE I've made your trip across the pond worth-
while, Damon," my father says that Saturday night at
our family seat in Kent outside London, leading the way
into the blue salon for drinks before dinner. His charm
offensive is in full swing, including that wide smile of his
and a conspiratorial tone. "I'm rather proud of it, I
admit."

"Plenty to be proud of, sir," Damon says.

"I'm sorry to see it go, but I trust you to give me a
fair price."

"I'll have to see what I can do." Damon wanders over
to the near wall, where a monstrosity of a dark and
gloomy Baroque oil painting depicts John the Baptist
losing his head (not my taste, art history major or not),
and takes a closer look. "I can give you a *great* price if
you want to part with some of those Picasso sketches."

My father chuckles. "That's the problem with you
Americans. Give you an inch, and you take the whole
continent. Admire your tenacity, though."

"You never know unless you try," Damon says with

an easy shrug and a flash of those dimples that makes my heartbeat skitter.

"Sit, sit." My father waves a hand as he settles on the main sofa. Damon sits in the chair to his right across the coffee table, and I sit in the chair to my father's left. Right on cue, a new member of staff—I don't know the woman's name yet—appears to take our drink orders. "What do you drink, Damon? I'm a whiskey man, myself."

"I have a taste for a dirty martini." Damon glances in my direction, the spark of mischief in his dark eyes belying his bland expression. If he finds it difficult to be on his best behavior for my father's benefit around me, he's not giving anything away. The bastard. "They're my new favorite. Thanks."

"A dirty martini," my father booms with delight, as though he gets a royalty every time anyone in the world drinks a dirty martini. I resist the urge to roll my eyes. It's been like this all afternoon, during lunch and our tour of the gallery. Everything Damon says and does seems to send my father into fits of ecstasy. As someone who also appreciates the finer points of Damon Black, I certainly understand this impulse. Still, if it gets any thicker in here, we'll all need to put on our Wellington boots to make our way through the shit. "Perfect. And you, Charlotte?"

The effort of not blushing, simpering or grinning at Damon in front of my father has consumed most of my energy for the day, especially with Damon's thrilling scent of incense and amber lingering in the air, keeping me high on hormones, so it takes a beat longer for me to peel my attention away from Damon than I would have liked.

"I'll have a martini as well," I tell my father. "Also dirty. Thanks."

"Lovely. The usual for me, dear," my father tells the staffer absently. I can tell by the subtle deflation of the woman's expression that she understands perfectly well that my father hasn't bothered to learn her name and probably never will. Still, she keeps her game face on. I give her credit for that and make a mental note to mention this to my father later. "And bring us some of those nibbly things I liked yesterday. Maybe a cheese plate."

"Right away, sir," the woman says, bustling off.

"You'll be comfortable in the guest house cottage tonight," my father tells Damon. "I'm sure you've already noticed that you have a great view of the rose garden and the fountain. That rose garden was my grandmother's—"

"Pardon me, sir," the staffer says, reappearing and then whispering something in my father's ear.

"Ah." My father beams at Damon and me. I wouldn't have thought that anything could make him happier than Damon's drink selection just now, but evidently, I was wrong. He pops up and trails the staffer to the doorway. "You'll excuse me for a moment, won't you? I need to have a quick word with someone."

They both disappear, their footsteps echoing down the hallway.

Leaving me alone with Damon for the first time today and the first time since he left my apartment the other night.

Our gazes connect across the length of the coffee table as he gets up and takes my father's seat on the sofa, supercharging the air and making my skin heat. He is focused. Intent. And the smoldering desire I see as he skims me up and down, his attention lingering on my legs, which are crossed and bare, and the hint of cleavage revealed by the square neck of my sleeveless navy dress, leaves me breathless and agitated inside my too-tight skin.

My condition is not helped by the fact that his absence from my days creates an exhausting new phenomenon that makes time slow down. I don't mean to sound like a lovesick teenager, but every hour without him now seems excruciating. Which means that the last several days have taken several years off my life, as has the constant spin of thoughts inside my foolish head.

Where is Damon right now? Who's he with? Is he thinking of me? Will he text soon? Call soon? Will he come on Saturday? Should I tell him that I've scheduled tea with my grandmother so I can tell her about my broken engagement while I'm here?

And the big one:

Does Damon think about me half as much as I think about him?

I can only pray that none of my growing obsession with him shows on my face.

And thank God that his lust for me finally shows on *his* after I've spent this whole long day with his impassive expression.

"How're you doing over there, princess?" he asks, leaning forward to rest his elbows on his knees, his voice silky.

"Very well, indeed." I mirror his position, knowing full well that it gives him a tantalizing view of my cleavage. "You?"

Sure enough, his attention dips. Lingers. Snags on my lips on the way back up to my eyes.

"Come over here and find out."

I study the look on his face. The chair. The sofas. It's not hard to imagine him taking me hard and fast against, say, the antique console in the corner before my father returns.

"I'm not sure that's a good idea," I tell him.

"It's a very bad idea. Come anyway."

Well, what can I say? It's not like the outcome was ever in any doubt.

I join him on the sofa, sitting as close as humanly possible without sitting on his lap. Like he did the night we met, he puts an arm around me, anchoring his hand on my opposite hip. Shifts me even closer. All without looking me in the eye. Then he takes my hand and presses a hard kiss to it, surprising me with his fervency. When his heated gaze finally flickers up to mine, I feel scorched.

Marked.

"You should stop looking at me like that," I murmur, running the backs of my fingers across his tender lips and enjoying his subtle shiver. "I can't very well fuck you on my father's sofa, can I?"

"We're perilously close to finding out. Did you talk to your grandmother yet?"

"I'm having tea with her on Thursday. Only time she was free."

He gives me a narrowed look as he keeps possession of my hand, lowering it to his thigh. "Don't fuck with me."

"Thursday."

"No further ties with Percy?"

"Well, he's texted me several times since the cocktail party. Hopefully, we'll be friends. We've always been friends if nothing else."

He nods, looking mollified. I enjoy the moment of quiet understanding between us, with nothing further needing to be said. It occurs to me that I'm poised to fall —and fall hard—for this man I barely know. It also occurs to me that I give zero cares.

"Did you miss me while I was gone, princess?"

I laugh. If only he knew how stupid a question he'd just asked. The inside of my brain has been plastered with his smile and laugh, his eyes, hair, body and everything else. Honestly, it looks like the walls inside the room of some teenage girl who's plastered images of the current boy band over every available inch.

I raise a brow. "Is my father fond of gilt?"

Damon grins that naughty and heart-stopping grin at me, all white teeth, dimples and sparkling eyes. And it occurs to me, not for the first time, that maybe I've already done a lot more falling than I thought.

He makes a show of looking around. Taking it all in. The stately home. The silk and chintz. The antiques, priceless art and fine rugs. The vases from several Chinese dynasties and the gilt on every frame and many tables and chairs.

"Well, it's nothing if not understated," he says, making me laugh hard enough to cause any nearby servants to peer around corners to see what's going on.

"I know. Imagine me trying to bring friends round from school for play dates."

"I imagine all your friends lived in similar houses," he says.

"Not true. Because my mom sent me to a school with lots of American kids so I'd be normal. How'd it work?"

"Didn't work at all. Nothing about you is normal."

Honestly, I feel like a hothouse orchid flourishing under all this attention.

"Don't flirt, sir. I know you're just trying to get laid."

There's that pirate's grin again. "Both things can be true. Am I trying to get laid? Yes. No secret there. Are you abnormally spectacular? Also yes." He glances around again, his expression turning wistful as he surveys the room. "I keep thinking about my father. He spent his entire life trying to achieve half the money, credibility and respect that your father has just because he was born a prince. If Pop could see me sitting here talking to a princess while surrounded with all this old money, he'd shit his pants."

The words cause a shadow to cross my heart. As a member of the royal family, I've spent more than my fair share of time questioning people's motives when they cozy up to me. The possibility that Damon might have an ulterior motive for pursuing me when I'm developing such strong feelings for him is more than I can stand.

"Is that why you're here with me now?" I ask, an edge creeping into my voice. "Settling your father's books? In the market for a trophy princess, are you?"

His entire body turns to ice right in front of me, starting from his expression down. It's like watching the birth of a North Atlantic glacier.

The transformation is unsettling.

"Absolutely," he says coldly. "That's the first thing I thought when you walked into Bemelmans. 'Damn. She's gorgeous. I sure want to fuck her. And, by the way, wouldn't it be great if she's *also* a princess?'"

"Damon—"

"Maybe *you* want to land a billionaire. The best billionaire. Should we talk about *that* possibility?"

I freeze, outraged by the implication even as I privately acknowledge that a man in his position is no doubt always concerned about opportunists. And God knows that if it was up to my father, he'd demand financial statements from both Percy and Damon, then happily hand me over to the one with the most zeros before the decimal point on his bottom line.

But while my father may be that person, *I* am not.

A glare-off ensues.

"There's not enough money in the world to saddle myself with a man I don't love for the rest of my life," I snap. "Don't be such an arse."

"Don't insult me with stupid questions."

"I'll do my best not to. But you can understand my concern."

"And you can understand mine."

"Are you going to shoot daggers from your eyeballs at me for the rest of the night?" I ask when he shows no signs of thawing out. "Maybe I should find my parka."

That steely gaze never wavers.

"I don't claim to know what's going on between us, princess. But it's *real*."

"Well, thank God for that," I say before I think better of it. "Since I'm about to take a rather large leap of faith in pursuing our relationship and I'd hate to wind up looking like a fool."

Those are evidently the magic words. He hesitates, jaw clenched and nostrils flaring. Then he blows out a breath, takes my face between his hands and pulls me close for a nuzzle and a whisper in my ear.

"I can't wait to be inside you again, Carly. I'm living for it."

Naturally, I melt into him.

"So am I."

The sound of approaching male voices breaks the spell between us, jarring me back to reality whether I want to go or not. Damon lets me go, and we share a regretful look as we hastily get up and return to our original seats. But the prickling electricity from our mutual attraction must linger in the air. Or maybe my burning cheeks give me away. Because my father's expression is a bit startled when he reenters, and Percy—oh, God, *Percy*; what's *he* doing here?—looks absolutely stricken as his smile fades and he studies the scene.

My father recovers first.

"Look who's popped in to join us for dinner, Charlotte," he says, recapturing his usual charm with evident difficulty. "Percy couldn't wait to see you once I mentioned you'd be in town, so I told him to come round."

Brilliant. My meddling father strikes again.

"Hi, Percy." I hastily stand and smooth my dress, flustered, before meeting him halfway for a double kiss on the cheeks. "This is a surprise."

"Clearly." Percy is usually the sweetest, most laid-back person in the room. Which makes the rough edge in his voice and tight jaw even more upsetting as he turns to Damon, who also stands, and extends a hand. "We meet again."

"We do indeed," Damon says grimly as they shake.

Damon and Percy don't take their eyes off each other. I've no idea what sorts of subliminal masculine messages volley between the two of them, but it makes dread trickle down my spine.

My father claps his hands in a valiant effort to act normal.

"What can we get you to drink, Percy? We started without you, but I think we can—"

"Forgive me, but I thought I detected a certain chemistry in the air just now." Percy splits his attention between me and Damon. I hate seeing that wounded look in his eyes beneath his anger. Percy doesn't deserve to be hurt. But knowing that and saving him from it are two different things. "Anything I need to know?"

10
CARLY

THE ONE THING that could make the upcoming conversation with Percy any worse would be to humiliate him by having it in front of this audience. So I babble the first thing that comes to mind.

"*Percy.* If you have a question for me, then we should discuss it privately—"

"Yeah," Damon quietly tells Percy. "*I* have something you should know."

"Pardon me?" I say with utter disbelief, trying to catch Damon's eye to shoot him a warning look.

But he focuses on Percy and ignores me. "We're adults," Damon continues. "You seem like a decent guy who deserves my honesty."

A sharp nod from Percy.

I, meanwhile, succumb to rising horror at the thought of everything Damon might be about to reveal. "*Damon…*"

I am universally ignored once again.

"I want Carly," Damon says lightly, as though he's

not lobbing a bomb into the middle of my hope to one day be friends with Percy. "She knows that. The ball's in her court."

I freeze, aghast. Maybe this is how Americans do things, but I'm positive Dad's sleepy blue salon hasn't seen a scene like this in generations, if ever.

Vivid color floods Percy's face. His lips thin out. "Got it. Thanks."

Damon turns to my father and extends his hand. "I'm going to skip dinner, sir. For obvious reasons. Maybe someone could send something to the cottage for me? We'll be in touch about the art. And I'll be out of your hair first thing in the morning. Thanks for the hospitality."

"Of course, Damon." My father works that handshake for all he's worth, going so far as to clap a hand on Damon's shoulder as if he's sending him off to the Crusades. "We'll be in touch."

For me? Damon spares a penetrating glance — nothing apologetic there, boy — as he strides off and takes all the air in the room with him, leaving me to my mess.

"Daddy," I bark, wishing I could grab the sword from the suit of armor in the corner and skewer him with it, "can Percy and I have the room, please? Thanks."

"Don't do anything hasty, Charlotte," he says, leaning in for a conciliatory kiss.

I lean out, turning my head. I'll deal with him in a minute. *"Thanks."*

My father squeezes Percy's shoulder on the way out, probably because he wants to treat both billionaires fairly, since they have even odds with me as far as he knows. But Percy looks stunned and seems not to notice.

Until my father quietly shuts the door on his way out and Percy stares me in the eye.

His expression? Devastated.

"Percy," I say helplessly, kicking myself for not just telling him about Damon to begin with and for continuing to communicate with Percy when he perceives my responses as mixed messages. What sort of genius gives a person false hope in the hopes of letting them down easy? When in the history of life has that ever worked out well? When did I become such a deluded idiot? "Can we sit down and talk, please?"

Bitter bark of laughter from Percy as he sits on the sofa. "We've been together for eight years, Carly. We've grown up together. Marriage was always at the end of our road. What are you doing? You can't just scuttle our entire relationship over a flirtation with some American."

Even in my ashamed and miserable state, I bristle at the implications that Damon is just some guy or that I'm foolish and immature enough to torpedo my entire future for a good fuck.

"That's not what I'm doing," I say sharply. "It's just that I've realized over the last few months that marriage wouldn't be right for us. I don't want to hurt you any worse, but I've got to be honest about my feelings."

He recoils. "Look. I don't even care what may or may not have happened between you two while we were on our break. If you wanted to sow some wild oats or get a rebellious phase out of your system, I'm not going to ask. I forgive you. We can get past it."

I want to clap a hand over his mouth. Stop him before he makes any further humiliating concessions that he'll regret later.

"Percy."

"But you can't just throw it all away, Carly. Not like this. Not without giving us a chance. I want this. Our parents want this. All our friends look at us as the golden couple—"

"Yes, but it's not right for *me*. Shouldn't that be part of the equation?"

"Yes, of course, but why isn't this right for you? Tell me *why*. Give me something I can understand."

I flounder, trying to get my words right.

"It's just that you and I have become more like comfortable old friends in the last year or so. I feel as though we've grown in different directions. We share friends, but not the same ideas or interests. There's no passion or excitement anymore."

"*I'm* passionate. *I'm* excited."

"I don't want to spend my life on a country estate doing charity work between having children. I mean, I want children, of course, but when I'm ready. After I've figured out my career and done the things I want to do in the world."

"If you want a career, have a career! I'm not stopping you! What is it that you want to do? You've never spoken of it."

"I want to stay in New York and paint," I admit. "And I'm not marrying the wrong man just because I'm out of school now and everyone else thinks it's the right time. I'm sorry, but I'm not."

He makes a nasty sound. Disbelieving. Derisive. Bitter.

"And I suppose you think Damon Black is the right man? You understand that he has a ruthless reputation in business, don't you?"

I stiffen.

He chokes back an ugly laugh.

"Of course I looked him up. Did you think I wouldn't after I saw the sparks between you at the cocktail party? I hope *you* have. He's never had a serious relationship. Goes through women the way you or I go through chips."

This, out of the entire painful conversation, is the very worst part. Because I've hurt a good and innocent man on my quest to structure the life I want and need. A life that I think might include Damon. Yet Percy has now drilled down to a hidden fear that I'd rather not acknowledge:

If given half a chance, Damon Black, whom I barely know, may well break my heart.

And I'm about to give him that chance because I won't be able to live with myself if I don't.

"I don't know what else to say, Percy," I say, staring at my hands as I rub them together, refusing to rise to his bait. "Other than you're a wonderful man. You've been a huge part of my life. An amazing part of my life. And I wouldn't be doing this if I weren't positive it was the right decision."

"For *you*."

"For both of us. Although I don't expect you to see that right now."

"Well, that's done, then," he says angrily. "You can't even look at me?"

I raise my eyes to his. Those familiar hazel eyes are hard. Unforgiving. Profoundly hurt and confused.

And I feel absolutely terrible for doing this to him. But also free. Ebullient.

Because this is not the man for me. He never was.

Just as I am not the woman for him and never could have been.

"I wish you the very best," I say from my heart.

"Sure you do. You know what? Fuck off. Fuck whoever you like."

With that, Percy walks out of the room, opening the door with a bang, and out of my life.

I can honestly say it's one of the worst moments of my life to see the simmering hatred as he goes. I'd hoped we could be friends. But at this moment I'm sure Percy would rather march me to the Tower and see if officials couldn't rethink the current policy against beheading.

I keep it together until I hear the distant slam of the front door. Then I rest my elbows on my knees and my head in my hands, emotionally exhausted and fighting tears.

This is how my father finds me a minute or two later.

"Charlotte? Is it over?"

I jerk my head up, fueled by sudden righteous anger. "What are you playing at? What the bloody hell do you think you're doing, inviting Percy here like that?"

My father shrugs, his expression mild and unrepentant. "He wanted to see you—"

"Because *you* told him I'd be here!"

"I wanted to give him a chance."

I stand, the better to yell at him. At this point, I don't even care if the staff hear.

"Yes, well, while *you're* manipulating things and moving chess pieces across your board, *I* was planning to try to be friends with him again. Now, thanks to you, that scene was twice as painful as it needed to be. I hope you're happy."

Another careless shrug. "I thought it might help keep

the men on their toes. Men like a good bit of competition."

"Competition?" I can barely spit the word out. "Is this a game to you? My happiness and Percy's feelings are, what? Monopoly money to you?"

"Course not, Charlotte. Why so dramatic?" He heads to the drink cart, pours himself a healthy whiskey and takes an appreciative sip. "But a girl has to be smart about these things. And I do hope you've thought through a strategy for dealing with Damon Black. If he's your choice. You could do much worse. Just don't blow it. Not when the family atmosphere is so toxic right now and I don't know where our funds are going to come from. We may well be cut off before it's all over."

"I don't need to depend on my dad or marry well to keep myself fed, thanks. I'll figure something out on my own."

"You'll *figure something out on your own*?" My father breaks into strangled laughter and barely gets his whiskey down without spewing it all over his priceless rugs. "You're delusional! Your dearly departed mother was so fond of making you out to be a regular child"—he pauses to make quotation marks with his fingers—"but where was she when it came to finances?"

I shift uncomfortably, knowing where this might be going, and try to head it off at the pass. "I can certainly—"

"No! You can't! You've never had a true *job*, Charlotte. You've had fun little internships because *I* called someone for you and pulled a string, but you've never had to work for a living like the average bloke. You take *my* credit card and pay for your rent and food, your clothes and your car. And then the invoice comes to *my* office and we pay for it. *That's* Monopoly money. D'you think for one second that you could afford your lifestyle without my deep pockets? D'you have any idea what your rent costs per month? Your petrol? Your *shoes*? And now you thumb your nose at Percy and march about saying you're going to be financially independent? I can hardly wait to see how you pull off this magical feat!"

"I'll figure something out!" I shout, gravely wounded by this overdose of the truth in all its brutality. Funny how I've never realized until this very second how bad my situation is. How grim my prospects are. I've spent my entire, largely aimless life skipping about while secure in the knowledge that there's an invisible safety net down there somewhere, ready to protect me if needed. If it wasn't my father, then it was Percy. I never bothered to formulate a Plan C.

But now I'm on my own with precious few skills and no experience.

And I'm in charge of weaving my own safety net.

My stomach churns at the prospect.

"I intend to paint," I add. "I told you that."

My father seems less than convinced about my chances of self-rescue as he shakes his head and regards me with open amusement.

"Not to put too fine a point on it, darling, but you're not the self-sufficient type. The best thing you can do for yourself is cozy up to Damon Black. You've brought one billionaire to heel. You can do it again."

This outdated sexist nonsense makes me apoplectic, as does his casual disregard of my feelings and my abilities. Money has nothing to do with my relationship with Damon—just as it had nothing to do with my relationship with Percy—and it never will.

My father's complete lack of faith in me is galling.

And motivating.

"Stay out of my life, Daddy. I'm warning you. I will handle Damon Black and the rest of my personal life without any help from you."

"I can hardly wait to see how you pull that rabbit out of your hat," he says, toasting me with his drink.

THIS IS JUST GREAT.

This is just. Fucking. Great.

I glance around the elegant confines of the so-called cottage (and, let me tell you, if this is a *cottage*, then my fifteen-million-dollar penthouse back in NYC is a *fixer-upper*), feeling like a lion trapped in a steamer trunk and wishing I could slash my way out. It's been two hours since I walked away from Carly and her unfolding domestic drama, and I've tried to deal with my surging adrenaline. *Tried*. I went for a five-mile jog on the paths around the manicured lawn and gardens of this insane estate. I came back, did roughly a hundred thousand push-ups and sit-ups because I was still strung tight, then showered. I ate the dinner they sent over for me, which now sits in my belly like a fifty-pound barbell.

Now here I am, sitting at the dining room table in my boxer briefs, staring blindly at my paperwork, getting steadily drunker by the second as I down the duke's whiskey, wonder what the hell Carly said and did with Percy and how I can find out one way or the other.

The one thing I won't do is pick up my phone and call her. My ridiculous pride is on the scene again, making an appearance like a meerkat poking its head out of a hole. And my pride says that since I already put it on the line for Carly—in front of an audience, no less—I need to sit and wait to see how this all unfolds. Be patient.

Too bad my pride doesn't know that I was only born with about one microgram of patience, and I used that all up in the first five minutes after I walked out earlier.

Carly, man. *Carly.*

I rest my elbows on the table, plant my face in my hands and rub my forehead hard enough to reveal my skull. She's got my balls in a pair of pliers, which I could deal with. It's the emotional roller coaster and the unshakable sensation of my thoughts and feelings being trapped in a blender that threaten to bring me to my knees.

It's having hope that we might get together again when, for all I know, she's now got Percy's engagement ring back on her finger and has forgotten about me picking my nose and waiting for her down here at the cottage.

Funny how I told her the other night that I went to her apartment because I wanted to see her in her natural habitat. What a fucking joke. *That* was a nice apartment. *This* is her natural habitat. Estates and servants. Priceless antiques and a father who's a duke. A grandmother who's a queen. A gilded life filled with the kinds of titles, privileges and wealth that a guy like me could only dream about. And yeah, my family and I have money. But it's wobbly and probably tacky new money, the kind that could still be yanked away or lost with one wrong move. My father demonstrated that. *This* money? *Carly's* money? It's been here for generations. Will be here for generations.

She belongs in this world. She and her father the duke.

And Percy. Let's not forget good old Percy, who was also to the manor born. Unlike me.

Funny how I felt so certain that *I'm* the guy for her. Not Percy.

But that was before I saw all *this*.

Let's get real. Part of me is wondering when security will show up and toss my ass out of here.

Sure, I've heard whispers about her dad's financial difficulties, but does that even matter when you're talking about a member of the royal family? Isn't this kind of wealth in your blood?

I don't have this. I can tell you that much. I can work my fingers to the bone and add that ninth zero to my bottom line this year, but I'll never have *this*.

My morale hits the negative digits.

Hell, I already knew I was punching above my weight when it came to Carly, and that was back when I thought she was a regular civilian woman. Now I know in my gut that I've got no chance. Why would she stick around for a loser like me when she could have this? Because I'm so special? Yeah, sure. I'm so special that I couldn't even get my own fucking mother to stick around.

But I want Carly.

I *want* her.

The idea that she might end up with some other guy

before I even get a real chance with her has me knotted with jealousy. That's not something I do. Jealousy? Me? Please. Why get jealous when your biggest ambition with any particular woman is a couple of hours of undiluted pleasure between the sheets? Isn't one sexy and experienced person roughly as good as any other?

So tell me why I'm just looking for an excuse to rip Percy to shreds and feed his fleshy remainder to the giant koi fish in the pond out yonder. Despite my impersonation of a semi-gracious person with him earlier.

The bottom line? I can't take much more of this uncertainty. Swear to God, I'm not cut out for it. I'll do whatever I have to do to get myself out of this purgatory of seething jealousy and uncertainty. I don't know what deceit, bribery, trickery or other nefarious activities I may need to engage in to get her to give me a real chance, but if she does, I swear I'll treat her like the princess she —

Knock-knock-knock.

Startled, I drop my hands. Cock my head and listen again.

Knock-knock-knock.

It's the front door. I jump up and hurry toward it, propelled by sudden excitement and that evil hope again. It seems like pride should make a token appearance at a moment like this, when I'm wearing my heart on my sleeve, my face and every other part of my body, but nope. Pride has finished its shift and clocked out for the night, leaving me alone with Carly and my wildest desires.

I throw the door open, and there she is. Wearing that sexy blue dress. With her hair down around her shoulders and her eyes sparkling. And sporting a seductive half-smile that lights up her face until it shines.

My heart leaps, making my breath catch.

I don't ask questions. When someone leaves a gift-wrapped and shrink-wrapped package of Benjamin Franklins on your front stoop, rings the doorbell and runs off, you don't ask questions. You just thank your lucky stars and start unwrapping.

So that's what I do.

I stoop just enough to wrap my arms around her waist, lift her straight up and swing her inside, nudging the door shut against the rest of the world and reveling in everything about her. Her triumphant laugh. Her warmth and strength as she presses closer and twines her arms around my neck. Her scent of lavender and the incendiary way she says my name, *"Damon,"* as though she's already coming for me when I know this thrilling night is just getting started.

I carry her down the world's longest hallway as fast as I can, the *thunk-thunk* of her heels as she kicks them off her feet urging me to go faster. Inside the bedroom, I loosen my hold just enough to flip the wall switch and light up the place with a few strategically placed lamps. No way am I missing the chance to see and appreciate every inch of this woman after I blew the opportunity the last time.

Then it's over to the bed, where I set her on her feet and rip back the covers to reveal pristine white sheets that seem to be waiting for us. She doesn't appreciate me opening any space between us and clings to my neck and shoulders the whole time, staring me in the face. I'm not gonna lie, it's easy to get drunk on this avid attention. I'm not worth it, but I'm not going to tell her that. Not when she acts like the secrets of the universe are hidden behind my eyes, if only she can see that far.

"Why are you looking at me like that?"

She hesitates, her color rising. "Did we imagine it, Damon? How good it was last time?"

This is the dumbest question imaginable, edging out *Will you build this skyscraper for free?* and *Would you mind if I murdered you right now?* by a mile.

"We didn't imagine anything."

I start to kiss her, but she cups my cheek and rubs her thumb across my lips, stopping me. "I'm so scared of you right now," she whispers.

I tense, hating the implication that I'd ever hurt her. In any way.

"Why?"

She pauses to get her thoughts together, and those big blue eyes are all I see. Wide. Uncertain. Achingly vulnerable.

"Because I know if I give you an inch, you'll take a mile. And I still want to give you that inch."

Listen, no one ever accused me of being emotionally intuitive, sensitive or even thoughtful. I'm a real estate guy. I understand building shit, financing shit and marketing shit. That's about it. So I have no fucking idea what she means by that. Only that it seems important to her. If she had the faintest idea of how she's possessed my brain since the second I met her, she'd stop wasting her own precious time with the insecurities.

But if she wants to talk about fear, I know from fear.

I grip her head on either side, catching handfuls of that silky hair.

"You want to know what scares *me*?" I swallow hard, my throat tight. "You walking out on me again."

Her eyes crinkle at the edges, hinting at a soft smile. "I'm not doing that."

"Make sure you don't. *Ever.*"

She shakes her head and pulls me in, thus ends the talking portion of the evening.

In my defense, I try to take it slow for her. My intention is to start out with one of those slow, gliding kisses, easing my way into her slick mouth with a few nuzzles and taking it from there. But her *lips*. They're so fucking plump and delicious. And her voluptuous tongue is already easing its way into *my* mouth. Just to really make my brain explode, she hits me with a sweet little coo, one of those helpless sounds of female encouragement that can fell a man faster than an elephant tranquilizer dart.

With that, rational thought leaves the building.

I groan and tighten my grip on her head, roughly tipping it back the way I need it, because I'm dying here. *Dying.* I kiss her deeper. Harder. Cry out with shock and pleasure when she nips me. Nip her back and laugh when she laughs. Catch her mouth again because I can't stand to let it go. Reach under her hair for her zipper. Stop because she's got a lot of hair.

"Turn around," I say, spinning her by the waist. Then she helps me shift all that hair over one shoulder, and I yank that zipper down to reveal her pale back with its dusting of coppery freckles, the band of her nude strapless bra and—be still my heart—the nude lace of her thong. I can't get that dress off her fast enough, especially when she helpfully pulls her arms free, bends and wiggles that ass in my face.

I can take a lot of things. Ass wiggling is not one of them.

I'm all over her, massaging and kissing my way down

her back as that dress falls to the floor and she kicks it aside. And what do you do with a juicy peach of an ass like this? You stroke it. You squeeze it as you ease those unwanted panties down her legs and out of your way. You bite it.

If her squealing and squirming are any indication, she likes that. A lot. So I slide my fingers down and stroke the insides of her thighs. Then I stroke that hot pussy from front to back and lick her juices off my fingers.

Mmmm. Delicious. Fresh oysters and womanly musk. Nirvana.

Just as I'm about to turn her around, back her onto the bed and settle one of her legs on my shoulder so I can have a good, long taste and hopefully also work her into a frenzy, she surprises me by turning to face me, a determined light in her eyes.

Oh, *shit*.

Goosebumps erupt all over me, race their way up my spine and collect at the nape of my neck.

"You know what I want?" she says huskily, staring me in the face as she rubs her hands down my belly and scrapes her nails back up, over my pecs. Down. Up. "I want to drive you out of your fucking mind."

Shaky laugh from me. "Mission accomplished, sweetheart."

"Not *quite*," she says, nimbly dropping to her knees in front of me.

This woman eases my boxers down my legs and off. Then she takes me deep inside the relentless suction of her mouth and, I'm telling you, it's game over. The visuals undo me as much as the sensations. The way her slick tongue rubs and works me. The way her cheeks suck in around me. The way those plump lips pucker around my head. The humming vibration from her victorious laugh as I moan her name and cup *her* head. The occasional flash of her eyes as she watches me and misses nothing.

Her glistening pink tongue. Her tongue. Her *tongue*.

The way it licks me from bottom to top, up one side and down the other. The way it circles my head, over and over again. The way it licks her lips as she stares up at me, confident in her skills and her ability to reduce me to a mindless hulk ruled by his rock-hard dick and surging hormones.

At some point, an existential crisis kicks in. I don't want the sweet torture to stop, for obvious reasons. On the other hand, her tender pussy needs some attention and I still don't know what color her nipples are.

And I am not giving her the last fucking word when it comes to driving people crazy.

So I step back, extracting myself from her mouth with some difficulty. Marvel at my ability to stand upright at all at this crucial juncture. Pull her up, push her back onto the bed and yank her forward by the hips until she's right where I want her.

Then I ease my way between her legs and settle her thighs on my shoulders.

"You know what *I* want, princess?"

"World peace?"

That dry British accent, especially in heated moments like this, kills me.

"Funny," I say, pressing my thumb to her clit hard enough to make her cry out as her hips jackknife off the bed. "I want to ruin you for anyone else. Ever again. How you like *that*?"

I lower my head without giving her a chance to respond and help myself to the sweetest and hottest pussy in the world. Every single inch of her slick cleft gets nuzzled, licked, tasted and savored. My skill set seems to meet with her approval. She gasps and squirms, writhing to get away while also holding my head in a death grip. Surrounded by the plump flesh of her thighs and saturated by the clean scent of her feminine musk, I'm sure that I've tapped into a direct line to heaven. God knows I'm not complaining if this is my last moment on earth.

On the other hand…

I've *still* never seen her nipples. And I really want her pussy to milk me dry when she comes.

So I surge to my feet, pausing to lick her navel and love on her lower belly before I straighten all the way up.

She never takes her eyes off me, greedy with anticipation.

I can't take my eyes off her. It takes me a long moment to savor her from head to toe and appreciate her shapely legs, manicured strip of red hair below her bikini line, heaving breasts hidden behind the cups of her strapless bra and all that pale skin, rosy now with desire. To watch as she slides back up the bed, settles with her head on the pillow and her hands massaging between her legs, picking up where I just left off.

She arches a brow. "Am I going to have to finish myself off?"

"Not on your life. Get rid of this," I say, reaching behind her to unhook the bra with a flick. I pull the thing free and watch, drunk with anticipation, as her soft breasts bounce into place and I glimpse her erect nipples for the first time. You'd think I just discovered that she's a fucking mermaid in disguise. "Ah, *shit*. They're coppery. Like your freckles."

Husky laugh from the princess. "Is that an important detail?"

Her amusement at my expense doesn't bother me. "Crucial. I'll have to come in for a closer look."

"By all means," she says, reaching for me. "The girls have been feeling quite neglected."

I would laugh, but my mouth has more important things to do. I stretch out on top of her and lick one nipple. Palm the other. Suck that first nipple. Massage the other. When she begins to shift restlessly and wraps her arms around my head to keep me close, I step up my game and work her harder. Switch sides. Press those amazing breasts together and make a sandwich out of my face.

It's no exaggeration to say that I wallow in her the way a starved pig wallows in his trough. I eat her up and swallow her whole.

I *worship* this woman, and that is not a word I've ever used before.

I snap out of my right mind and into some altered state where the only things that matter are giving equal mouth time to those hard little beads and seeing how high her rising cries can go. How hard she can scratch my back. How fast her hips can pump.

My sweaty face and torso, trembling arms and straining dick don't matter. My needs don't matter. Only *she* matters.

So when she yanks on my hair and says, "Stop, Damon. I need you inside me," I don't think twice.

What's there to think about when I can see the naked heat in her eyes and hear the raw urgency in her voice? When she opens her legs and cocks her hips for me?

Intentions don't get any clearer than that, folks.

Making some crazy feral sound that rightfully belongs in an Animal Planet documentary, I take my dick in hand, move it to her core and enter her in a single hard stroke.

12

DAMON

"DAMON."

I'm levered up on my elbows, so I have the perfect view of her face. I'll never forget the astonishment in her expression or the dewiness of her plump berry lips as they ease into the sultry smile of a woman who's getting exactly what she wants and needs. The way her chest rises and falls against mine. Those pointy nipples. The way her thighs immediately rise to grip my hips.

I'll never get over how tight her pussy is. How slick. How fucking *hot*.

"I want a million years of this," I say, beginning to move. "Just so you know."

There may have been a triumphant laugh from her, but hell, I don't know. I'm not in my right mind. My right mind and I aren't even on the same continent.

All I know is that I fuck her long and hard and she gives as good as she gets. She grabs my head and pulls me in, demanding my mouth. Kisses me until I can't breathe and don't care about breathing. She treats my ass to a few stinging slaps, giving me encouragement that

I don't need. She sighs and moans. Whispers frantic things that I can't quite hear.

This goes on and on, until the wet smacks between our sweaty bodies threaten to drown out our voices. Her name becomes my mantra, pouring out of my mouth repeatedly. There may be some other stuff jumbled in there, words about how hot she is. How amazing. How ridiculously *sexy*. Who can say?

My lower back begins to ache from my thrusting hips, but that doesn't matter. My burning thighs don't matter.

The only thing that matters?

Driving. Her. Fucking. Insane.

My reward comes when she stiffens and arches beneath me, her voice rising in a single high note of anguished pleasure. I lock my muscles, determined to keep her there in that suspended ecstasy for as long as possible. Not until she eases down and starts to catch her breath after several beats do I rev up my hips again, thrusting hard enough against her sweet spot to make her body spasm and her cries multiply exponentially.

Only when I'm sure that she's given me all she's got do I let myself go to where my body drives me. I thrust harder and harder, shouting her name.

And I wouldn't say that I finally come. What do you call it when the orgasm is ripped from your body, leaving you shattered and ruined?

What's the word for *that*?

By now my arms are aching with exertion. My thighs are rubber. I don't want to crush her, so I ease to my side, taking her with me and feeling an inexplicable stab of disappointment when I pull out.

That's when it hits me.

For the first in my life, I just had unplanned unprotected sex.

I lie there, stunned, as the realization sinks in.

First, what the *fuck*?

Second, a woman in Carly's position doesn't need the scandal of an unwed pregnancy. Her father the duke and her grandmother the Queen won't thank her for embarrassing the family, and that's on top of the fact that her stated plans for her life don't include a kid at this point. She and I are barely starting to get our act together with each other. She's counting on me to protect her. She can't very well learn to trust me if I let my hormones poison my judgment every time she walks in the room.

You need to do better by her, asshole.

Third, and I'm surprised at how distant a consideration this is, a man in my position needs to protect his own fool self. The world is full of billionaire baby mama wannabees. Not that Carly's in that category or ever would be. She's not after my money. I know that in my bones.

Still. I always wear condoms. *Always*.

She stirs next to me. I reflexively tighten my grip to keep her close.

"I wasn't aware that we were trying to become parents and share all our various rashes, warts and sores," comes that wry voice, drowsy now as she smooths her hair out of her face and looks up at me. "Luckily, I'm on the pill, so you don't need to worry about becoming a father in nine months. But we should do better next time. Don't you think?"

I blink, the words sinking in.

So we didn't just make a kid. Good to know. Great news. I never much saw myself as the fatherly type anyway. Not after the way my parents burned our family to the ground on their way to a divorce decree.

Wonder why this dose of common sense just pricked my euphoric bubble?

Why do I feel like a dormant caveman just woke inside me, rolled over and found his club?

"We're not using condoms." The steely note in my tone makes me sound like pharaoh commanding the Egyptians to double their daily quotient of bricks, but I can't seem to help it. "I can get you a report from my doctor saying I'm clean if you want. But we're not using condoms. Not after that."

I stare her in the face, challenging her to say something about it. Daring her.

"You won't be so smug if I turn up pregnant, will you?" she says.

I tell myself to keep my big, fat mouth shut, but my big, fat mouth isn't listening.

"You royals have the ability to read people's minds?" I say, sudden tension—what the fuck is my problem right now? I'm in bed with a woman talking about *kids*?— killing off a good portion of my post-sex relaxation. "Good to know."

She looks at me as though I'm crazy. Which I clearly am.

"Tomorrow I'm going to pretend I didn't hear any of this. I'm assuming that sex has scrambled your brain and you are not in your rational mind right now."

"You and rational don't coexist with me," I say flatly. "That should be evident by now."

She takes a closer look at me, frowning. "Why do you say it like it's a bad thing?" she asks.

I open my mouth and fumble for the appropriate

answer. One that will let her know this is getting serious on my end but give her no clue exactly how serious. Even *I* have no idea how serious this thing could get. I just know that it's not looking remotely casual from where I'm standing.

"Because I get the feeling my life is changing," I confess. "Not sure how I feel about that."

"My life is also changing, in case you hadn't noticed," she says tartly. "Yet you're the only one glaring as though someone has threatened you with a cricket bat."

I feel a surge of admiration and exasperation for this woman. They often travel together where she's concerned.

"Do you have to call me out on everything, princess? Every single time?"

"Yes."

"That takes some getting used to," I tell her.

"Sorry about that."

I raise my brows. "Sure you are."

We grin together for a delicious moment that sweeps away the unexpected weirdness just now. I hate to rock the boat again so soon, but there's something I need to know.

I open my mouth, determined to tread carefully.

"How did things go with Percy? You okay?"

She quickly looks away, her smile already a thing of the past. "I don't want to talk about Percy when I'm in bed with you," she says, adjusting the linens. "Or ever, come to that."

"Indulge me."

Now she goes to work fluffing the pillows and leaning against them. Anything to avoid my gaze, I suppose.

"I didn't deny being with you. It's for the best."

"I agree," I tell her. "But the question is how you feel about it. And it would be great if you could look me in the eye when you answer."

Exasperated sigh from Carly, but she does resume eye contact. Reluctantly.

I brace for the worst. Something about how she and Percy agreed to take a break and see other people but plan to reconnect in a few months or a year to reevaluate their relationship and future.

But that's not what she says.

"Percy's not the man for me. I realize that now. End of story."

I study her closely, determined to catch any flicker of her eyelid or tic in her jaw. Anything to tell me that she's either lying to herself or to me. If any parts of her are still hung up on that guy, I need to know before this goes any further and I get my guts ripped out and stomped into oblivion the way my father once did. Even at this early stage of the proceedings, I recognize that Carly is eminently capable of leaving me for dead.

To my immense gratitude, there's nothing secretive in her steady gaze. Just enough open honesty and warmth for me to suspect that I can trust her.

What a thrilling thought *that* is.

My chest eases, letting go of the breath I didn't know I'd been holding.

"That answer makes me happy, princess," I say, sudden emotion making my voice hoarse. "Really happy."

She cups my face and leans in for a soft kiss that I return with interest. "I'm really glad to hear that. Since your happiness is starting to matter to me." She hesitates. Flashes a rueful smile. "A lot."

Neither of us speak for a beat or two, the silence expanding into something that feels a lot like mutual understanding.

Until my big, fat mouth pipes up again.

"If there's any reason I should put the brakes on this relationship, tell me now, Carly. Before I get in too deep. Stop looking at me like I'm crazy. I'm dead serious."

Sultry smile from the sex goddess. Which doesn't exactly reassure me.

But I'm not mad at her when she comes in for another little kiss and infuses it with a generous helping of tongue this time. Matter of fact, I'm fucking light-headed and giddy. And my dick? Never better.

"You don't think I'm letting you go now that I have my hooks in you nice and deep, do you?" she purrs, her wide eyes the picture of angelic innocence.

"Fuck," I say, leaping on her like a rabid hyena, yanking the linens down to reveal those pointy nipples and rolling her beneath me again.

She squeals with laughter and delight, all the encouragement I need.

Another round of no-holds-barred fucking—aloof and proper Princess Charlotte is a fan of doggy style, I discover—is more than my poor heart and body can take. I pass out when it's over, sprawled spread-eagled on my belly and too exhausted to even cover us up.

Then I succumb to a raging case of PTSD when the morning chill wakes me, and I discover she's gone once again when I reach for her.

"Carly," I call, sitting bolt upright and groggily trying

to come up to speed on weak sunlight filtering through the strange room. *"Carly."*

There's no part of me that exercises common sense and recognizes that a) she's probably in the bathroom; and b) I can probably track her down again because I'm on her family estate. Only a greased pipeline directly to the scared-shitless ten-year-old kid who went to bed one night with a mother and woke the next morning to discover that she'd walked out of what was left of my childhood without the courtesy of a note.

"No need to wake the dead," Carly says, looking bemused as she appears in the doorway with a gray ball of fur in one hand and a steaming cup of tea in the other. "I'm right here."

I feel a tsunami of relief. Now that I'm fully awake, I realize I might have overreacted. But tell that to my pounding heart.

"What the hell are you doing?" I rest against the pillows and rub my eyes, mostly to disguise how shaken I am. "Wandering around in the middle the night."

"I wasn't *wandering*, grumble bunny. The cat wanted to come in, so I let her in. Then my thoughts started going and I couldn't sleep, so I made tea. I assume that's still legal?"

"After that stunt you pulled last time? Your privileges have been revoked. You need to go to the bathroom? You leave me a sticky note on your pillow."

For a second, I think she's going to rip me a new one for barking out orders, but then she surprises me. Like she always does.

"Damon," she says softly. "Try to pay attention. I would have thought that my last conversation with my former boyfriend and/or my screaming orgasms last night would give you a clue, but you're evidently not as bright as I'd hoped. So I'll spell it out for you. I'm crazy about your amazing cock. Almost as crazy as I am about *you*. All that means that I'm not going anywhere. Okay?"

I grunt something indistinct, which is the best I can manage from this emotional roller coaster she's got me on. Awkward, but what do you expect? One second, I think she's pulled another disappearing act. The next, she's making me wonder whether it might be possible for me to convince her to fall in love with me.

Which is insane, because love and I don't have a long history together. Take my word for it.

She starts to smile. Stifles it.

"Friends?"

"No," I snap. "I like your cat, though. What's her name?"

"Her name is Weasel," she says proudly, then presses a kiss to the cat's furry head before dropping her onto the bed. The cat, who has vivid green eyes, immediately creeps forward to check me out. "Because she likes to slink around in the shadows and sneak up on everybody."

"How're you doing, kitty?" I say, scratching her ears and generating an enthusiastic round of purring. "Are you a good girl?"

"She *is* a good girl." Carly plops down on the edge of the bed. Sips her tea. "I love her to death. I keep begging my father to let her live with me, but he can't bear to part with her."

"Ah. That's why you want your own cat."

"Yes, exactly," she says, tickling the cat's belly and making her squirm. "And it's a good thing you get along with cats. Or else you'd be out on your arse."

"Thank God for small favors," I say, watching her closely. "So why were your thoughts going at this ungodly hour?"

Her expression falls. "Because my father keeps issuing dire warnings about cutting me off and me needing to figure out how to make my way in the world," she says glumly. "And it's belatedly dawned on me that loving art and making a living in art as a painter are two different things. I have my degrees now, but what good are they? It was all fine and good when the plan was for me to marry Percy and retire to the country to pop out a few children. But in terms of being able to afford New York City? Stay in my current apartment? I should have just majored in underwater chalk drawing and been done with it."

My brain automatically spins into problem-solving mode, which is normal.

But it's tinged with a powerful new protective instinct that, let me assure you, is *not* normal.

What follows? A string of increasingly insane ideas.

I know people in the art world. I should make a few calls for her. See if someone could help her get started in her career.

Better yet, I could buy a gallery for her so she could exhibit her own work.

That could work, right?

As for her expenses in the meantime, why not give her my credit card?

As for her apartment, I'll just cover her rent for her.

Better yet, I'll just buy the apartment and give it to her.

No, wait.

We'll be spending a lot of time together once we get back to the city, right? Why does she need an apartment at all? I live in a massive penthouse. She should just move in with me. All problems solved. I'll cover her housing and expenses and she'll never have to work if she doesn't want to.

Done.

My mouth is opening to triumphantly announce that I have the solution and say all of this to her when some modicum of common sense finally grinds and cranks its way into gear.

She. Should. Just. Move. In. With. Me.

Did I just think that? Did I just *mean* that?

Yeah, I realize with a jolt. *You bet your ass I did.*

Still mean it, as a matter of fact. Worse? The only thing keeping me from saying it is my fear that I'll scare her away if I come on too strong.

But Carly living with me?

Yeah, man. I want one of those.

For now, I borrow against my stores of self-control for decades to come, rub my hands over the top of my head and force myself to impersonate a normal human man who's just begun to date a woman he likes.

"So, what, ah," I say, then pause to clear my throat. "What are your thoughts?"

"Not sure yet," she says thoughtfully, blithely unaware of the existential crisis brewing inside me. "Obviously, I've got some contacts I need to reach out to. And I did get a couple of offers to work in galleries before I graduated, but I turned them down because I thought I'd be moving back home. Maybe I should check in with them again. I'd love a steady salary while I work on my painting on the side until it takes off. Assuming it takes off. Anyway, you don't want to hear all this right now."

Yeah. Yeah, I do.

"I mean…" I shrug, trying to look nonchalant. "I'm here if you want to talk. Kick around some ideas."

She brightens, her delighted smile lighting me up in a way the sun never could.

"Really? That means a lot. I know you've got your career together. And have done for a long time. I hope you have patience with me while I flounder about."

"I'll see what I can do," I say wryly.

"Good. I'm going to think things through. I've got an idea, but I want to make a proper plan before I discuss it with you. So you won't think I'm a complete idiot."

"Never, princess."

She pecks me on the cheek, then pops up like she's late for a meeting. My semi-hard morning dick is having none of that. I grab her wrist, being careful of her tea.

"There you go again," I say. "Knock it off."

"Oh, no you don't," she says, correctly reading my thoughts. "I'm going for a jog. You're welcome to come with me if you like. The grounds are amazing."

"I *do* like," I say, surprised and delighted. "But what about your dad and the staff? You don't care about them seeing us together at the crack o'dawn?"

"Course not," she says, scowling. "What do you Americans say? Grown-ass? I'm a grown-ass woman. It's *my* life."

"Works for me," I say, stifling a laugh. "But aren't you afraid the staff will blab to some tabloid?"

The suggestion seems to shock her. "No. My father has everyone sign their souls away in confidentiality agreements. And these are mostly people who've been with the family for years."

"Well, if you're cool with us going public, you're welcome to hop a ride back on my jet. Whenever we're ready to go. I just need to be back in time for my Monday morning meeting."

"Oh, but I'm still spending time with Granny on Thursday, remember? You'll have to go back without me."

Not exactly the end of the world, but the reminder still hits me like a thirty-pound bag of concrete dropped on my foot. I have the wild impulse to ask if she's insane. Because why else would she think I could stagger all the way to the end of the week without her?

"Thursday?"

"Yes, but my flight's on Friday."

"Friday?"

"You'll be fine, darling," she says, laughing at the look on my face. "I know you can barely imagine a second without me, but you'll soldier on."

I'm not entirely sure I will. And she's right. The seconds without her sure seem a hell of a lot longer than the seconds with her in them.

But we're both here now. And I plan to make the most of it.

"We'll have to stockpile some orgasms for our time apart, then," I say, then I take the tea, set it on the night-stand with a *thunk* and pull her back into bed with me and the cat.

13

CARLY

I DIAL Damon's number as soon as I arrive back in my apartment that Friday evening, tossing my keys and my stack of accumulated mail on the foyer console and kicking my sandals into their basket. These transatlantic flights are always hell on my neck and shoulders, so I lean my head back and forth, trying to work out some of the kinks.

"You home?" he asks before the phone manages a single full ring.

I can't stop my grin. We've talked and texted all week, but he's no better at hiding his eagerness to see me again than I am at hiding mine.

"Well, hello to you too. Just walked in."

"On my way."

"Hang on," I say quickly. "Give me an hour or so, because my friend Michele is on her way and I haven't seen her for—"

But the line is already dead.

"Unbelievable," I mutter.

I'm still laughing over his impatience when my phone rings.

"It's me," Michele says when I answer.

"Come on up," I say, buzzing her in.

We squeal with girlish delight when she appears in my doorway, carrying on the way we did when we both got high marks on our first sketches back in freshman composition. I consider her my best-friend soul mate, probably because she doesn't give two fucks about my royal status and has never hesitated to tell me the unvarnished truth in all its messy detail. It's been about a month since I've seen her, during which time she's reworked her braids into a bun on top of her head. Her ivory linen sundress highlights her perfect skin, which is the beautiful color of the finest English toffee, and her dimpled smile threatens to swallow her entire face.

"You look *amazing*, you gorgeous witch," I tell her when I finally let her go and steer her over to the sofa, where we settle. "All glowing and summery. While *I* look rumpled and pathetic."

"Stop the nonsense. Like *you're* not wearing a great dress." She flaps a hand at my coral maxi dress. "Love the wavy hair. Glad you finally started listening to me about not straightening it all the time."

I try to disguise my blush by tucking my hair behind my ear, deciding that now is not the moment to mention that Damon's comments about my hair, not hers, are responsible for the change.

"Well, it's much less work. That's for sure."

"So how's Granny? What did she send me?"

Michele has traveled back home with me several times over the years, spending breaks and vacations at our various homes. She and my grandmother have become thick as thieves, bonding over their shared love of yappy little dogs and Kentucky bourbon.

I roll my eyes. "Don't pretend you don't see the big tin of Scottish shortbread sitting right there on the coffee table waiting for you."

"Perfect!" She claps her hands, then tucks into the shortbread with gusto. "And don't expect me to share."

"Wouldn't dream of it. I've already eaten my body weight in shortbread this week, anyway. So I'm off it now."

"Good. Before I forget to mention it, I told the landlord to add you to the lease next month," she says around crunches. "I can't wait to have you back in the studio with me. The band is back together!"

Michele is an accomplished portraitist and has started making quite a name for herself among the Upper East Side set, all of whom are eager to pay top dollar for paintings of their little darlings and furry children.

"I know. I'm so keen to start painting again. I can't tell you. I'll be moving all my supplies and canvases back to the studio. And getting some things out of storage. Oh, and framing some of the older paintings."

"Good deal. Are you excited about this new chapter of your life?"

"Yes. Well, I'm scared to pieces about trying to make my own way financially."

"Aren't we all, sister?"

"True enough," I say, laughing. "But some of us have had more practice at it than others."

"Also true. But now you'll know what it feels like to make your own way. I think it'll be good for you. You'll be so proud of yourself to be the captain of your own ship."

"Assuming I don't run my ship aground," I say darkly.

"I'm not saying there won't be a learning curve, but you've got a good plan. You can do it. If *I* can do it, *you* can do it."

"From your lips to God's ears."

"So what's going on with Percy? Please tell me you dropped his ass for once and for all."

I frown. "Well, I did, but you don't have to say it like *that*."

She pulls a blank look that fools no one. "Like *what*? Like I've been telling you for years that being with him is like watching white paint dry?"

There's nothing like a hearty *I told you so* to make one feel foolish. Had I listened to Michele years ago, the final break with Percy wouldn't have been nearly as painful. Certainly, there would've been no engagement to break.

"Percy's a lovely person," I say, stung. "I could have done much worse. He'll make someone a wonderful husband."

"As long as that *someone* isn't you. You do realize he's only able to talk about three things, right? Soccer, rugby and whatever organic farming breakthroughs they've made on his estate that season."

"And salmon fishing," I add, trying not to smile. "He's quite conversant in salmon fishing."

"True," she says.

"I just think we should have the proper respect for a kind person whose heart I just broke."

"RIP, Percy," she says solemnly, bowing her head and pressing a hand to her heart.

"Much better," I say, reaching for a piece of shortbread.

Michele smacks my hand away. "So what made you pull the plug?"

"I had a, ah, moment of clarity," I say, feeling that same heat in my cheeks again and deciding that now is not the time to mention that Damon's cock was instrumental in helping me decide.

But Michele, being Michele, seems to know. She gasps, eyes widening, and lowers her piece of shortbread from her mouth.

"Hang on," she says, assessing me with that shrewd gaze of hers. "You met someone, didn't you? I see all the signs. You've been out of touch. Sexy new hair style. Bright eyes. Pink cheeks. Final break with Percy. What the hell is going on? Tell mama."

Obviously, no one can withstand this sort of withering cross-examination. Least of all me.

My blush intensifies, threatening to melt me and send the entire sofa up in flames. There's no stopping my grin. And I find myself categorically unable to look her in the eye.

"It's *nothing*," I say, covering my face with both hands before I humiliate myself any further. "Only, you may be right. I *may* have met someone."

"And fucked him too, by the look of it," she says with horrified fascination, because she knows how out of character this is for me.

"Michele!"

"Who is he?" she demands around her scandalized grin.

"His name is Damon Black," I say with as much dignity as I can muster. Which is none, to be honest. "I met him at Bemelmans the night you skivved off on me."

"I had cramps!"

"Well, it's still your fault."

"Damon Black," she says, dusting the crumbs from her hands and reaching for her phone. "Why is that name ringing a bell?"

"He's in real estate."

"That's right." She snaps her fingers, then taps away on the phone. "Here he is. Wow. Gorgeous. Page Six likes to comment on his active social life. You know that, don't you?"

"I *don't* know that," I say sourly, snatching the phone from her and peeking, much to my immediate regret. A quick skim reveals that if she's beautiful, accomplished, photogenic and, presumably, great in bed, Damon will date her. Jealousy consumes me. Ridiculous? Yes, but there you have it. I'm no slouch, but tell that to my plummeting morale. "Thanks for that," I say, thrusting the phone back at her.

"Don't act brand-new," she says, shrugging. "You know a man like *that* has a past."

"Yes, well, knowing about it as a vague theory is entirely different to seeing it right there in front of me in all its high-def glory."

"So? What's he like?" she says, laughing at my pain. "Please tell me he's more interesting than Percy."

"*Much.*"

My fervency snags her attention. Those brown eyes of hers narrow again, watching me closely. "You like him."

"Obviously," I say, putting my entire soul into maintaining some decorum and not simpering.

"No, you *really* like him."

It's all fun and games until that moment when your best friend stares you in the face, sees through your bravado and realizes that the stakes are higher than you'd like to admit, even to yourself. That emotions are involved. That things are getting unexpectedly complicated.

"I really like him," I say softly. "It's sort of scary how much I like him, to be honest."

Michele, being Michele, nods with infinite under-standing. "*Please* tell me he's a good person. I'd hate to have to kick a billionaire's ass. You know he has the money to bribe the authorities to send me to prison for life."

We laugh long and hard, the sudden tension broken.

"So? Tell me something about him," she says.

"You'll see for yourself in a minute. He's on his way."

"Really? I'd better study up on him, then," she says, bending her head over her phone and scrolling furiously.

I shake my head at her and take the opportunity to check my own phone, which is full to bursting with noti-fications about missed calls, texts and emails while I was on the plane. I scan and listen, then lower my phone, dumbstruck.

"Oh my God."

Michele's head snaps up. "What?"

"I've got"—I do another quick count, unable to believe my eyes—"*eight* people reaching out wanting to set up meetings about hiring me for their various artistic projects and enterprises. Some of which I'm not even qualified for. They're all gushing like I've turned into Pablo Picasso overnight."

"Well, there you go," she says, beaming at me. "Great job spreading the word that you're available. Your career's already off to a great start."

"No, Michele. There I *don't* go. I haven't put out the

word. I wanted more time to think things through and formulate my business plan. Which means someone else put out the word for me."

"Your father," she says, scowling. As my longtime best friend, she's had a front-row seat to my father's interference and manipulations over the years.

Much as I'd love to pin the tail on the overbearing paternal figure, I've got a funny feeling about this.

"You don't think… You don't think *Damon* did this, do you?"

"How the hell would I know?" she says, shrugging. "I've never met the man. And isn't this a good thing if he did? Why are you all frowned up like that?"

Good question, Carly. Why *are* you all frowned up?

I take my time, staring off in the distance and struggling to put my grievance into words.

"Because I didn't ask him to take up for me. I was sort of looking forward to doing this for myself. I've always relied on my father to smooth the way for me. And then he wanted to marry me off to Percy, so *he* could smooth the way for me. Now *this*." I flick my attention back to Michele, my frown deepening. "What's with these men? Don't they think I can do anything by myself?"

"Don't get your panties in a bunch. *I* have complete confidence in you, but you can't blame *them* for wanting to make sure you're okay. You don't have a long history of doing things for yourself. Sorry, but you don't."

See? What did I tell you about Michele? The unvarnished truth in all its messy detail.

"That's about to change," I say firmly. I'm discovering, much to my surprise, that nothing motivates me like being underestimated and wanting to prove someone wrong. "I'm going to do this myself. You just watch."

"Like I said, I'm on *your* side," she says, holding her hands up in a pretend surrender. "So don't come at —"

The buzzer buzzes.

"That's him," I say, getting up as my heart rate pounds double time.

"Okay, well, don't freak out on him," she says. "It's a nice thing he did. Right?"

"Can't decide whether it was nice or controlling. Like my father," I say, hurrying off.

By the time Damon gets off the elevator and begins the long approach to my apartment, incredibly handsome in his dark suit and power tie, I almost don't care. I've missed him so much this week. I'm *so* thrilled to see him. And that's before I see that his arms are full of brown bags of some sort of delicious-smelling takeout and a bouquet of the most exquisite pale pink flowers — hydrangea, roses, orchids and innumerable others, at a glance — to welcome me back.

As for the look on his face?

Quiet intensity. Smoldering desire. Banked joy.

He plans to eat me alive at the first opportunity.

I plan to let him.

But I can't let him know how ecstatic I am to see him again after less than a week. I've lived a perfectly pleasant existence without him my entire life. Several days without him won't turn me into a clingy mess. Not if I can help it.

That being the case, it seems imperative for me to tamp down all my enthusiasm and repress most of my smile as I relieve him of the flowers and usher him inside.

"Ah, yes," I say, watching him set the takeout bags on

the console and noting the overnight bag slung over his shoulder with great interest as he drops it to the floor. "You just made a quick stop at the nearest five-star restaurant and luxury florist on your way over. As one does for a casual Friday night at home. Yet you don't seem to be wearing your tuxedo?"

He laughs, already reaching for me. "One is glad to see you," he says, pulling me into his arms. "One wants to make sure you know it."

The ferocity of his hug takes my breath away, as does his exhilarating scent of incense and amber. Which is strange, because I also feel as though everything is now okay again, and I can truly breathe for the first time since we went our separate ways the other day. For a moment I think he plans to back me against the nearest wall and fuck me right there, it's that intense. It crosses my mind to warn him that we're not alone. It also crosses my mind to tell Michele to excuse us for a moment and lock herself in the bathroom until we tell her it's safe to come out.

But then his touch slides into tenderness, catching me by surprise as we sway together. He presses his lips and his fingers deep into my hair. His thumbs stroke the sides of my face and neck. My arms are wrapped tight around his waist beneath his jacket, the perfect position for them to feel the way his lungs expand as he inhales my scent. He murmurs something raw and urgent, something precious, and I kick myself for not being able to hear it.

I wonder if maybe he's beginning to feel—or could one day feel, if I play my cards right and don't blow it—the way I feel about him. Which is that my life was fine before I met him, but it's sure starting to feel like it's never going to be spectacular without him.

He gives me a final kiss on the forehead, then loosens his grip enough to look down at my face. "Hi."

"Hi."

"Miss me?" he asks, his voice husky.

"Oh, were you gone?"

All the glowing warmth in his expression quickly transforms into a look of flinty determination.

"Just so you know? I know what that is. That's you trying to keep me at arm's length."

As always, his intuitive ability to successfully identify my feelings startles me.

"And every time you do that, it makes me more motivated—and I'm already a highly motivated guy—to make sure you fall crazy in love with me," he continues. "Fair warning."

I open my mouth, not that I have any possible response to that pronouncement, but a merciful new interruption saves me.

"Is that Damon?" Michele calls from the living room.

"It *is*," I say.

Damon's brows go up. "You didn't tell me you had company."

"You haven't given me much of a chance, have you?" I say, taking his hand and steering him through the foyer and into the living room, where Michele stands to greet him. "You'd better brace yourself and be on your best behavior. It's my best friend, Michele."

"Hello, best friend Michele," he says with an easy grin as he extends his hand. The effect is dazzling, and that smile isn't even directed at me. "Pleasure."

Michele blinks. I know her well enough to see her private battle with a surge of hormones as she tries to decide whether to swoon outright, but, to her credit, she recovers quickly.

"Damon Black," she says with her usual glimmer of mischief. "You're just in time. I was just researching you. It's my responsibility, since I ride or die with Carly. Obviously, you get demerits for being wildly unattractive."

Damon smothers a startled laugh. "So I'm off to a bad start."

"Very bad." Michele flaps a hand at her phone. "I also see that you've got bad credit—"

Damon and I burst into laughter.

"—and women seem to like you a *little* too much. So I'm not sure that I can recommend you to Carly," she concludes gravely.

"How can I dig myself out of this hole?" he responds with equal gravity.

"Well, you've got a firm handshake. Plus, you brought flowers and food. So points for being thoughtful," she says brightly.

"And there's enough food for *you*," Damon points out, making himself comfortable on the sofa.

"More points. But I'm going to leave you two love-birds alone while I go home to read your criminal background check and work on your dossier. Also, I'm going to say a little prayer for you, because I kind of like you and hope you stick around. But Carly doesn't like over-bearing men. She gets enough of that with her father. Word to the wise."

"Got it," Damon says with a vague frown and a puzzled look in my direction that Michele doesn't seem to notice. "Hope to see you again."

"You too." Michele turns to me for a quick hug. "Love you."

"Love you too. I'll call you tomorrow."

"Sounds good."

With that, she lets herself out, leaving me alone with Damon and a sudden awkward silence as I join him on the sofa and try to gather my thoughts.

14

CARLY

HE TAKES off his jacket and tie and lays them across the nearest chair before rolling up his shirt sleeves, small domestic gestures that provoke a powerful response inside me. It's almost like he's home with me. Well, he *is* home with me, clearly, but it feels like his home is *with* me.

"Everything okay?" he asks quietly.

"Course," I say in my best impression of carefree nonchalance. My thoughts aren't completely together, and I'd rather not get into it with him until they are. I can't decide whether I should ask him about the women or the networking first, or whether I should mention any of it at all. The one thing I'm determined not to do? Tell him about the lump of jealousy that's sitting heavy in my chest right now.

"Good," he says before resting his ankle on his knee, folding his hands in his lap and watching me, waiting.

I shift uncomfortably. Flip my hair off my shoulders because it seems to be getting hot in here. Struggle with my words. Come up with nothing.

"Because if it's about the women I've dated…"

"Yes, and what a rich and varied assortment of them you've had," I snap before I can stop myself. "You've applied yourself with gusto, haven't you?"

One corner of his mouth twitches with unmistakable amusement, the bastard. "Not that you're jealous."

"Don't be ridiculous."

"Good. I'm sure you recognize that those women are in my past, so it would be a waste of your time and energy to be jealous."

I try to be satisfied with that reassurance, but the silence and his steady gaze unnerve me. As does the primitive power of my jealousy. Which is, I admit, something I've never felt before.

"Only there did seem to be such a large number of them. A simple calculation based on your age and the number of pictures I saw would seem to indicate that you hook up with a new woman approximately every 2.4 days. I'm sure my clock is already running down."

He laughs. *Laughs.*

"What's so bloody *funny*?" I snarl.

"Where should I start?" he says, leaning his elbow on the back of the sofa and resting his head on his hand. "With the fact that the most exciting woman I've ever met thinks she has something to be jealous about?"

I blink, startled.

"With the fact that you're jealous about insignificant relationships that don't begin to compare with what you and I have already built? Or how about the fact that whatever you're feeling can't be a millionth of what I feel when I remember how close you came to marrying someone who belongs in your world better than I do?"

We stare at each other, my heart thumping as I

absorb both his words and the reluctant vulnerability in his expression.

"You make it hard to maintain a good sulk," I tell him.

"Why sulk?" He gently takes a strand of my hair, wraps it around his fingers and lets it slip back into place. "I already told you once. What we did before doesn't matter. You were with Percy. I was with…everybody."

I let out a startled laugh.

His expression softens until the warmth in his smiling eyes could best be described as naked adoration. It makes my heart melt.

"None of that matters now, princess. Does it?"

I think about the time spent with Percy, for which I'm grateful. My experience with him taught me what it's like to be loved by a good man and took me from girl to woman.

Then I think about how alive, excited, hopeful and special I feel when Damon looks at me like *that*.

Absolutely no comparison.

"No," I say. "Doesn't matter. Not at all."

He takes my hair again. Tugs me in for a kiss that's sweetly lingering. Infinitely promising.

"Anything else?" His heavy-lidded eyes are all I can see. "We've got a reunion to get to."

I hate to rock our precious boat at a moment like this, but it can't be helped. My newfound independence is too important to me.

"One other thing," I say, pulling back. "Everyone in the New York art world seems to suddenly think I'm the best thing since Andy Warhol. No one can live without me. They all want to throw money and opportunities at me. Did you have anything to do with that?"

He hesitates, looking wary. Probably something in my tone.

"Depends. Will my answer affect my chances of getting laid in the next five minutes?"

"Wow. Brilliant. At this point, you're in trouble no matter how you answer," I say, glaring.

Aggrieved sigh from Damon. "I know some people. I made a few calls on your behalf. I wanted to help."

Unbelievable. Is that how the male mind works?

"I appreciate the thoughtful gesture, but did you ever stop to wonder whether I *wanted* your help?"

"Yeah, actually." He roughly rubs the top of his head, rumpling his hair. "I briefly wondered, then I did it anyway. I probably should've listened to my gut instinct. At least I didn't lease a studio for you or buy you an art gallery. Which I thought about."

"An *art gallery*?" I squawk. "What planet are you from?"

"One where I clearly don't understand the rules. What's the problem? Help me out."

"The *problem*?" I say, growing more heated by the second. "The problem is that you either don't care about the plans I've made for myself or think I'm incapable of making plans for myself. And in the process, you've no doubt made everyone wonder whether I'm sleeping my way to the top of the art world. So thanks for that."

"Stop trying to put things in the worst possible light."

"Oh, is *that* what I'm doing?"

"Yes. First, we're together now. If people don't realize it yet, they will soon. Second, networking makes the world go round. I'm surprised you don't know that, given your background and status—"

"Yes, I *do* know that, and that's exactly why—"

"Finally," he says loudly, "of course I think you're capable of making plans for yourself. But if I can smooth the way for you and make your path easier, I'm going to do that. I want you to be successful beyond your wildest dreams. I've got all these resources. What do you think they're for?"

"Am I allowed to speak now?"

"Absolutely."

"Lovely," I say acidly. "It might interest you to know that I'm quite looking forward to running my own life. My mother tried to give me a normal life, but my father and the family made that pretty much impossible. Decisions were handed down from on high about what schools I could attend—"

"Everyone gets told what school they're going to, princess."

"—what camps I could attend and which friends I could have. Hobbies, clothes, hair, makeup. You name it, it was all overseen by my father with an eye toward making sure I never embarrassed the family. One time, I wanted to get a part-time job with my friends at a pet-grooming salon, but he refused because, and this is a direct quote, 'the optics are bad.' And you should've seen the fight we had when I insisted on going to NYU instead of Cambridge. That was pretty much the first and only time I stood up for myself."

Damon stills, looking stricken.

"I've had enough of being managed and suffocated and arranged like some Barbie doll inside her princess house. It's *my* life. *I'll* make the decisions."

"Of course it's your life. No one's arguing about that."

"Well, thank God."

"But I'm here now. It's my job to make life easier for you and to protect you."

Something inside me snaps, unleashing my full temper.

"I just told you I'm not a doll! *I* will take care of myself even if no one I know thinks I can! No one hired you to protect me!"

The words are still ringing through the air when the realization hits me that I may have gone too far and crossed the line into hurtful.

And that's *before* I see him recoil as though I've just whacked him across the face with his beautiful bouquet of flowers.

"No one…*hired* me?" he asks, his voice deathly quiet.

I can't back-pedal fast enough. "Obviously, I didn't mean—"

"Help me out with that one, princess. Are you telling me not to care about you? Because—news flash—I don't need your permission for that."

"I'm sorry. This is all new to me."

"That makes two of us."

"I just… I know people think of me as a spoiled princess."

He frowns. "What people? Not me."

"A lot of people. It's a dismissive attitude people have. They don't think I'll be around for long. My teachers were always surprised when I worked hard and applied myself in school. My father's biggest ambition was to marry me off to Percy. It's like no one expects much from me. And I never expected that much for myself, to be truthful. I've certainly never been fully in charge of my own life. But I am now. Do you want to hear my plans?"

"Of course I want to hear," he says, leaning in.

"Okay," I say, suddenly nervous. Here I am with my silly little half-formed career path talking to a titan of his industry. I'd hate for him to realize what a flake I am this early in our relationship. "I've got a huge stockpile of paintings from school. I'm going to sell them online. I've already commissioned someone to build my website and help with my social media presence. I'll work with a broker to begin with, but the world of selling art online is really growing. I think I might be able to—"

"Brilliant."

"—grow my presence— Wait, what?"

"Brilliant."

I breathe into an ecstatic and relieved grin. "Really?"

"Really. But there are a lot of issues. Do you want to incorporate, or not? What about sales taxes? What kind of commission do these brokers command? Will that be worth it? You need a lawyer. You'll need safe but inexpensive shipping—"

"I know, I know," I say, the enormity of my task starting to sink in. "I'm already working on it."

"And what about a studio? You'll need space for all this."

"Well, that's one good thing," I say happily. "I'm signing on to share space with Michele. She's got a huge studio."

"Well done, princess," he says. "When will all this launch?"

"Hopefully the first of the year."

"Good. What can I do?"

"I don't know," I say, now surprised and pleased by his willingness to help. Which was probably the reaction he expected in the first place. "I really appreciate the offer, though. Let me think about it."

"I want to make sure you have everything you need. Like I said, I know people. I can snap my fingers and it's all done."

"I'm beginning to see why you're at the top of your game," I say with amused exasperation. "You're relentless. Only maybe wait until I get a chance to think about it and get back to you before you start snapping your fingers like a genie."

He scowls. "Fuck that. Give me a task. It's against my nature to sit around doing nothing."

I laugh at his intensity. "You're exhausting."

"You have no idea," he says. "So…?"

"For right now? I plan to take a quick shower, since I smell like the inside of the British Airways cabin. I'd love a massage after that to help me unwind. If you're any good with your hands?"

He dimples, the slight narrowing of his eyes telling me he's heard my challenge and plans to overcome it in spectacular fashion.

"That I can do," he says, giving me a smoldering once-over.

"Did we just successfully navigate our first fight?" I ask. "I feel like the occasion calls for a plaque or a toast or something."

"I think I can scrounge up some champagne from the goodies I brought," he says, grinning as he stands and offers a hand to pull me up. "And I don't like the term *fight*. We disagreed. We worked through it. That's what adults do."

"I don't care what you call it, darling," I say happily, bobbing up to kiss his cheek before I head to my shower. "As long as you still love me."

He gets the funniest look on his face. Along the lines of what you'd expect to see if someone stuck their fork in a plug and jiggled.

I roll my eyes. Honestly, *men*. One mention of *love* or *marriage* in their presence, even peripherally, and most of them start looking at you as though you approached them with your garden gloves to suggest a rectal exam. I've seen it a million times with my girlfriends and their significant others.

"No need to look at me like that," I say tartly before the poor man launches himself into cardiac arrest. "I was only joking."

But he only manages a faint smile as he turns away, his expression shadowed.

Luckily, he seems to have recovered by the time I emerge from the shower a few minutes later, towel-wrapped and sweet smelling with my hair piled in a messy bun. He's waiting for me in my bedroom, with the bed turned down, a candle lit on the nightstand and two fizzing flutes of champagne on standby. Most importantly? He's sprawled against the pillows with one knee bent, stripped down to his black boxer briefs, revealing the body that catapults me to the edge of orgasm every time I see it. Broad, muscular shoulders, arms and torso, every groove of his abs beautifully artic-ulated. Powerful thighs and toned calves. The bulge of his cock, noticeable even when it's not standing at full attention.

There's something deliciously disconcerting about seeing him here, in my private inner sanctum, in all his masculine glory. Like seeing a bull in the bra section of Victoria's Secret.

"I see you've successfully found the bed," I say, startling him.

He lowers his phone and puts it on the nightstand, taking his time in giving me a thorough once-over. I'm still partially wet, with water droplets dotting my shoulders and cleavage above the white towel. My bare legs receive special attention, as do my manicured feet in my fancy little flip-flops. By the time his gaze flicks back to my face, it's white-hot.

"I scoped out your bed the other night when I was here."

"I remember," I say sourly, walking toward him as he stands. "I was rather hoping you'd put it to good use that night. I was an incredibly sad girl when you left."

"I plan to make up for that tonight," he says, reaching under the pillow and presenting me with a white envelope.

I open it, bemused. "You're not serving me with legal papers, are you?"

"Nope. Just my clean medical report."

I give it a glance, then set it on the nightstand, touched that he'd go to such lengths to reassure me.

"Thanks. You didn't have to do that, though. You gave your word. I would've trusted you. I wouldn't be sleeping with you if I didn't trust you to some extent."

"Right," he says, his unblinking and unsmiling attention focused on my face. "But I want you to *trust* me."

"Oh," I say, not at all sure what to make of that. Our relationship keeps making these incremental steps toward significance, and I can't quite decide whether to let it happen as the most natural thing in the world or throw up a few barriers to protect myself. And I *do* trust him, down deep on some invisible and illogical cellular level. I'm surprised by how much I trust him.

Luckily, now is not the time for analysis.

"Let's go," he says, gesturing toward the bed. "I'm dying to get my hands on you."

The tent at the front of his boxer briefs leaves no doubt about that and makes me involuntarily lick my lips.

"*Fuck*, princess," he says, adjusting himself with a shaky laugh. "Give me half a chance here."

Delighted as I am to see that I have that effect on him, I give him a wide berth as I walk the final step or two to the bed, thinking that my massage might be at risk if I venture too close, but he's a perfect gentleman. I push the pillows aside and spare him a glance over my shoulder (I have his avid attention, no question) before I open the towel in the front. I take a leisurely sip of the champagne, which is crisp and delicious. Then I make sure I remain covered to his eyes as I stretch out on my belly on the bed, resting my chin on my arms.

"Any areas that need special attention?" he asks, his voice thick as he comes to stand over me.

"I'm sure you'll figure that out," I say, sighing as I let my eyes roll closed.

"I look forward to it."

With that, the maestro picks up his baton and plays me a symphony. His magical hands start at my shoulders and work every tired muscle with strong, rhythmic squeezes. He finds and loosens knots that I didn't know I had, eliciting X-rated groans of pleasure from me. I know I sound like some manic adult entertainment star, but I swear I can't help myself when he gets anywhere near me. He attends to my back, arms and fingers. He leans into my thighs and kneads my calves until my bones turn to molten gold, no doubt ruining my ability to ever walk again. Not that I care. He gets hold of my feet and exploits hidden pressure points that send zings of electrifying sensation directly to my pussy. He takes a battering ram to all my body's tensions, leaving me both relaxed and energized. Reborn.

And *then*…

The towel slowly slips down the length of my body, further sensitizing my overheated flesh with its nubbly texture as it trails over my thighs and the backs of my knees and disappears.

My shiver of anticipation turns to an adrenaline surge when a long moment of nothing follows. He's far too quiet. Far too still. And I know this is going to be *good*.

What can I say? When I'm right, I'm right.

His fingers gently brush aside a few strands of hair from my neck, then his mouth makes its grand entrance for the evening. It nips and nuzzles its way to the special place where neck curves into shoulder. I coo helplessly, a sexual puppet dancing on the end of his string. That's intense enough. But then his mouth firms, his tongue enters the picture and I lose my fucking mind.

I don't even know how to describe what he does to me, and it's even more intense because no other part of his body touches me. To say that he kissed my neck would be like saying oceans tend to be damp. And of course Damon Black never does anything halfway. He's probably genetically incapable of doing anything half-way. He…he…*makes love* to that tender hollow, the secret bundle of nerve endings that's the key to any woman's secret garden if her partner only takes the time to turn it.

And I *sob* with ecstasy. Tears and everything. Something—let me assure you—I've never done before.

Until his mouth skates up to my ear, his voice hoarse. Urgent. "You know I want to fuck you, princess."

"Fuck me," I whisper desperately, still lost amid my ugly cry. *"Please."*

There's no further warning. Just the rough grip of his hands on my hips as he both pulls me up to all fours and drags me to the edge of the bed. Rarely has a woman cocked her hips and spread herself wide with such abandon. It's as though someone has set a doomsday clock on me and I will meet my ultimate destruction unless he is buried to the hilt inside me within the next second.

Eager to oblige, he enters me with a single hard thrust that makes us both cry out. He pumps relentlessly, his hard body slapping against mine *exactly* the way I need it to. His cock unerringly hitting the exact right spot inside me. I bear down, tightening all my inner muscles around him and laughing when he groans helplessly. But retaliation is swift. One of his hands leaves my hips and heads straight to my dangling breasts for an endless round of squeezing and nipple rubbing. His other hand? Straight to the vee between my legs, where his strong fingers exert the exact right pressure on my clit.

He punctuates every thrust with a mantra whispered in his ragged voice.

"I missed you, Carly… Missed you… *Missed you.*"

He gives me everything he's got, and I reward him with a strangled shout as I experience the biggest, brightest, longest and most electrifyingly intense orgasm of my life.

He joins me immediately, my name pouring out of his mouth as our bodies spasm together. There's a suspended moment out of time where we linger in the sensation, wringing every drop of pleasure from each other's bodies before we collapse together. The end result? Me on my belly with him still inside me and his arms still around me. Him half on top of me. Both sets of legs sticking off the side of the bed.

I don't know how long we lie there before both a chill and my sudden embarrassment set in. All I know is that he suddenly pulls away and stands. I take the opportunity to hastily wipe away the tears lingering on my cheeks, cover myself with the sheet and try to find some composure.

But composure is thin on the ground today.

For a second, I think he's going to leave without a word, which is fine with me. I need a minute to catch my breath and process what just happened, because whatever it was? It wasn't normal. It's not normal for me to give and lose myself with such wild abandon, even when Damon touches me. It's not normal for me to experience this searing certainty that my life has irrevocably changed, and the old Carly is gone forever, for good or for bad. Because I'll be the happiest woman in the world if he sticks around. And the pathetic image of heartbreak if he doesn't.

But he pauses at the door. Hesitates without looking directly at me, no more eager to make eye contact at this awkward moment than I am.

"You'll be okay," he says quietly.

"What?" I say, startled because I think for one horrified beat that he's just read my mind.

"With your, ah, plan. To, ah, sell your art. You're

amazing. You're going to do great. With my help or without it. No doubt in my mind. And I didn't mean to, ah, come on too strong."

This unqualified endorsement and near-apology catch me completely off guard. I risk a glance at his face. Our gazes connect for one blistering second, during which I somehow manage to notice everything about him. His sweaty face and torso, high color and unreadable eyes. The remnants of his erection, which leave his cock ruddy and engorged. The shell-shocked expression that perfectly mirrors what I'm feeling inside.

And I have to wonder whether his half-apology refers to his unsolicited career help or what just happened in this bed.

Either way, I discover that I don't need to hear it. I also discover that it's too soon for me to look him in the face.

"It's okay," I say, quickly turning away to adjust the pillows behind me.

There's a pause. He clears his throat.

"I'm just going to, ah…"

He trails off, his footsteps retreating down the hallway to the bathroom.

Leaving me to collapse on the bed stare up at the ceiling and wonder if I've been foolish enough—and rash enough—to fall crazy in love with a man I'm only just beginning to know.

15

DAMON

AS LONG AS you still love me.

Seven months later and Carly's throwaway line still chimes through my head at inconvenient and unsettling moments, demanding my attention. Like it wants something from me. Too bad I have nothing to give. Especially on a night like tonight, when my nerves are already frayed and raw from waiting on news about this fucking deal. Ryker is in the middle of a Hail Mary meeting in Tokyo this very second, but it's not looking good. I've already missed my self-imposed year-end deadline to make the billionaire club, but I've spent the last couple of weeks assuring myself that it can happen first quarter. But the longer the minutes tick by without word from Ryker, the more convinced I become that my dream is up in smoke. For the foreseeable future, anyway.

So my mood could best be described as tense and shitty as I do a lap around my penthouse, straightening up before Carly gets here in a couple of minutes, and that's just for starters.

Here's where it really gets good. This cold and

gloomy January evening is also the twenty-fifth anniversary of the night my mother chose my father's best friend over my father and walked out of our lives without a word to me or my brothers. We went to bed the night before with a mother who kissed us good night like always, told us she loved us and acted like she gave a fuck about us, then woke in the morning to my heartbroken and vengeful father and the rattle of lonely clothes hangers in her empty closet.

I think about her sometimes.

I wonder if we might have seen her again and reconciled if she hadn't gotten herself killed in that car accident a few months later, when their custody case was in full swing. I wonder what she'd think about Carly. Whether she'd want grandchildren.

Tonight, I even went so far as to dig the old shot of her on the beach out of my drawer and give it a glance. A mistake, obviously. The sight of her happy and carefree, with her long sandy hair blowing and her hazel eyes sparkling, only ever intensifies that dull ache in my chest. That's why I've never framed the fucking photo and put it out where I can see it.

I don't want to get upset every time I see her face. And she doesn't deserve a place of honor in my memories, my apartment or my life, anyway.

This time of year, when the days are short, the streets are slushy and my nerves are edgy, always reminds me of the one formative lesson that she taught me:

You can't trust anybody. Especially the people you'd most like to trust.

As long as you still love me.

I don't believe in romantic love. Never have. My parents' nasty divorce blasted the word and the idea right out of my vocabulary. And if, on the off chance that it *does* exist, it exists for other people. People who have a heart for a heart rather than a smoking crater where their heart used to be.

Which raises the question: what the fuck do I think I'm doing with Carly? Why have I greedily absorbed every second with her these last months? Why does the smoking crater in the dead center of my chest also ache when I think about her and when she's not with me?

Why the *fuck* did I give her a key to my penthouse within a month of our officially getting together?

Why do I feel this insane push-pull when it comes to her? It's as though there's an elephant inside me that belongs to her and I spent half my time trying to push it toward her and the other half trying to yank it back.

Here's the biggie:

Why did I just happen to wander by Harry Winston this afternoon and, worse, just happen to glance at the engagement rings? Because today is also Carly's birthday? That excuse doesn't really cut it. Not when I've planned her gift—and it's spectacular, if I say so myself—for weeks and currently have it waiting for her in the bedroom.

I don't believe in love. I'm never getting married. Those two facts about me will never change.

Even if the ongoing effort of keeping Carly at some sort of emotional arm's-length feels like swallowing a spoonful of steaming dog shit and trying to keep it down. Impossible.

Drained, I sink onto one end of the sectional and let my unfocused gaze slip to my gauzy curtains, which blur the glinting skyline and river. Like my thoughts, I suppose. God knows I'm not seeing straight right now.

Luckily, my buzzing phone snaps me out of my weird altered state. It's Ryker.

"Yeah," I say, the knot in my gut tightening. "What's happening?"

"No dice. It's over. I'm on my way to the airport now."

"Shit," I say, using my free hand to rub my forehead hard enough to make the flesh fall off. "Seven months of wasted effort."

"Yeah, well. You win some, you lose some. And tomorrow's another day, Scarlett O'Hara."

"Fuck that. I've got goals to accomplish."

"You and me both."

I sit there as the silence turns brittle, my mood plummeting to subterranean levels. So our deal fell through. Happens sometimes. I won't get that additional zero to add to my net worth by my thirty-fifth birthday. Big fucking whoop. The goal was always a stretch, not to mention the fact that it was self-imposed. What harm is there in not making this extra cheddar right now? It's not as though I need it. It's not as though anyone needs this kind of money. It's not as though someone is on their way to evict me from the penthouse right now and force me to live in a van down by the river. We'll try again. God knows we didn't get this far by giving up.

But…

It's all tied together in my mind. Me. The deal. The money.

Carly.

Deserving Carly. Being worthy of Carly.

Self-destructive thoughts creep into my head. Those fuckers always show up at the worst possible time.

Good old Percy's got ancient family money, doesn't he, man?

He's *not a fucking loser like* you *are, is he?*

I catch myself. Rub my head again and try to snap out of it.

Carly will be here soon. I don't want her to see me like this. Not on her birthday, of all days.

I think about how hard she's worked to get her online store up and running in the last several months. The hours she's spent in the studio. The meetings with web designers, photographers and framers. Have I helped here and there? Yeah, sure. I provide support. Guidance. But that's about it. Carly has put herself into this project, heart and soul. When it takes off and becomes a huge success, as I know it will, it will be entirely because of her own efforts.

I can't get over how hard she works. I can't believe how proud I am of her.

I think about her launch party tomorrow. She'll be the star of her own show on her own merits, something she deserves.

Meanwhile, *I'm* such a gem that I wasted months of my time trying to get this worthless deal together.

Yeah, sure, man. You're exactly *the type of guy Carly deserves.*

Fucking loser.

"Well, anyway, I'll call you when I get back," my brother says.

"Yep."

Something in my voice tips him off, which is one of those annoying things about brothers. They hear shit you'd rather keep hidden.

"What gives? Do I need to put you on suicide watch?" he says.

"Couple things on my mind. That's all."

"It's not Carly, is it?" he asks sharply. "Don't go messing that up. She's good for you."

Good for me.

I stifle a snort. *Good for me* doesn't exactly cut it in terms of showing the whole picture. Oxygen is good for me too, but you need to slide it over into the *essential* category.

I start thinking again because, hey, why not? I'm already tied up in knots, right? How much worse could it get?

I think about how much my life has changed since she walked into it. On Carly's watch? I laugh. I relax. I unwind. I still work, like always, but I also *live*. I smile when she shows up. I go to sleep smiling. I wake up smiling. The loss of this deal has just kicked me and my brothers in the teeth, but Carly will be here soon, and I will smile again. As long as she's around? I have an endless supply of smiles.

A glance around illustrates her presence in a dozen different ways here in this contemporary cavern I call home.

The fluffy blue cashmere throw that showed up one day because she said all the black leather was too cold. The matching throw pillows. The plants. The hardcover mysteries now stacked on the coffee table. The electric glass teakettle in the kitchen with its blue light as the water boils. The tea and biscuit tins. Her running shoes lined up next to mine in the foyer closet.

Her slinky nightgown under my pillows.

Her mysterious lotions, hair products and makeup in the bathroom.

Her eyes. Her *laugh*.

Funny to see all the ways she's warmed this place up

and remember how I thought she was an ice princess when I first met her. Unbelievable, actually.

Have I fucked it up and caused her to walk out on me yet? Not yet. But I'm sure I will.

"It's her birthday today." I eyeball the bucket of champagne I have icing on the counter next to a massive bouquet of flowers for the birthday girl. "I'm taking her to dinner when she gets home from the studio in a minute."

"Good. Don't do too much navel gazing. I know how you get this time of year. You get yourself into a funk over Christmas and start thinking about Mom—"

The mention of the M-word makes me edgier. The very last thing I need is to discuss her with Ryker at this unsettled moment. I don't need some deep analysis, especially from my younger brother. Fortunately, the jingle of keys and sound of the door opening give me the excuse I need to head this off at the pass.

"Here's Carly now," I say, standing just as she peeks around the corner and beams at the sight of me. "I'll get back to you."

"Wish her happy birthday for me."

"Will do."

I hang up and toss the phone aside, smiling already.

See? What did I tell you?

"Hello," she says, bringing enough brightness with her to blast away both the night's gloom outside and the emotional gloom in my head. "And what are you doing home so early, sir? You're trying to put together an important deal. You can't skip out early."

"I've got an important birthday to celebrate. Get over here, birthday girl."

"Not so fast," she says, lingering in the archway. "Was that Ryker? How did his meeting go?"

I manage to keep my game face on and my smile in place. Tonight is her night.

"We're not discussing work right now. Mine or yours. Am I getting a kiss or not? And before you answer, fair warning: no kiss, no gift. And I got you a great gift."

"I *see* that," she says, all aglow as she eyeballs the flowers. She takes off her coat and tosses it on the nearest chair, revealing jeans and a sweater. "Thank you for the gorgeous bouquet."

"That's not your present, silly girl," I say, pleased with myself. That's another thing she does for me: makes me feel like something special on a regular basis. "Well, it's not your *real* present. What are you doing? I'm getting the feeling you're hiding something over there."

"I *am* hiding something," she says, clapping with excitement before disappearing back into the foyer. "Stay where you are. I've got a present for you."

"For *me*? It's not *my* birthday."

"Yes, but it's much more fun to give presents on your birthday than it is to receive them. Here we are."

And she makes a grand re-entrance holding a large, flat package that's been wrapped in brown paper. Something that could only be one of her paintings.

"For *me*?" I say, stunned as she hurries over and leans it against the coffee table.

"Yes, *you*. Do you see anyone else standing here? Hurry up. Open it!"

Her thoughtfulness catches me by surprise, as does the sudden well of emotion in my throat. I discover that I don't want to open the gift right now. Or maybe it's more accurate to say I'm afraid of how much this gesture means to me. She's already shaping up to be the greatest human being I've ever met. I can't take one more reason for her to mean the world to me. There's just no room inside me for another big or turbulent emotion.

But she's waiting. Watching me.

I swallow as much of my fear as I can manage and give her a quick kiss.

"Thank you, sweetheart."

"Don't thank me until you've seen it," she says, laughing.

Her enthusiasm is contagious. I tear through the paper with no idea what to expect, because she can paint anything if she has her acrylic paints and canvas. Landscapes. Still lifes. Portraits. Abstracts. But this is...this is...

"I call it *Joie*," she tells me, sounding nervous now. *Joy* in French. "I hope you like it."

"*Like* it?" I say, which is all I can manage.

She has, once again, taken my breath and blown my mind. I should be used to it by now. But getting used to Carly's presence in my life would be like getting used to a panda moving into your guest bedroom. You do your best and maybe grab some bamboo on your way home, but there's no real preparing for it.

The best way for me to describe it would be if someone took an abstract painting of a heart and pixelated it. Smudged it. If the painting contained every warm and wonderful color anybody ever saw. All the golds, yellows and fiery reds. All the lovely blues and greens. If you ever saw a color and thought, *Wow, that's gorgeous*, that color is in this painting.

And that painting leaps out at me, grabs me and makes me happy.

The same way this woman has grabbed me. And made me ecstatically happy.

I think about how seamlessly we've woven our lives together, splitting our time between here and her place. I try to figure out if maybe there's some hidden part of me that wants to take the limits off this relationship and trust her that last little bit. Which is why I can't speak. I'm too busy pressing my lips together and pretending I have control over my emotions. Too busy wondering if this is her way of telling me that she's fallen in love with me, because *she* probably believes in love even if *I* don't.

Too busy doubting whether my luck could ever get that good.

"I just wanted you to have something to thank you for all of your support and help," she says quietly, staring me in the face. "And to let you know…how much it means to me."

How much *it* means to her.

Not how much *I* mean to her.

Something inside me notes the distinction with a tiny stab of disappointment.

There? See? Just like I thought. My luck could never get that good. I have a statistically better chance of winning the lotto while being abducted by an alien spaceship while it's being struck by lightning than I do of making Carly fall for me.

You want to know the funny thing?

For a cynical non-believer like me, that's a surprisingly bitter pill to swallow.

16

DAMON

BUT I NOD, grateful for the gift anyway, and pull her in for a hug. A lingering kiss to her forehead.

That seems to satisfy her.

"You like it?" she asks brightly as I turn her loose.

"Yep," I say gruffly. "Thanks."

"You're welcome, darling."

The tenderness in the D-word sticks it to me good. I decide to take myself out of the situation for a minute or two before I completely lose it.

"Time for *your* present," I say, standing and turning toward the bedroom.

"I feel as though I've already had it." She flops onto the sectional and settles in with unmitigated delight, kicking up her legs. "A successful gift. Flowers. Champagne. Dinner. Probably an amazing fucking later —"

"You can count on that last part," I say over my shoulder.

"— and now another present. I'm a very lucky girl, aren't I? *Oh, what is it?*"

I return with a smug grin and a giant lidded basket

topped with a blue satin bow, which I carefully place on the coffee table in front of her as I resume my seat. The faint mewling and scuffling inside the box give away the whole surprise, but who cares? She's already given me the exact dumbstruck look—wide-eyed and slack-jawed —that I was hoping for.

"You *didn't*," she says.

"One way to find out," I say, shrugging.

Repressing a squeal, she yanks the ribbon loose and tosses the lid aside. Out pops the sorriest excuse for a cat that I could find at the local shelter. Black with a white muzzle and paws, he's underweight, has patches of missing fur and an ear that looks as though some passing dog took a bite out of it. He's even got a crazy *meow* that sounds more like a *rowowow*. But, to his credit, he's got bright green eyes and a winning personality that includes a hearty purr and the ability to stand up on his hind legs and put his front paws around people's necks in an enthusiastic feline hug.

"Oh my God, Damon," she says, gasping as though I've presented her with some sleek new kitten from the latest designer cat breeder. "It's a mangy used cat!"

"It is," I say with immense satisfaction. "He's got a skin condition, but that's clearing up. He's also gaining weight now that they've put him on some new food. I wanted to get you a nice, fresh cat from a certified breeder, but I figured that would get me in trouble for ignoring all the needy neighborhood cats. And I plan to get laid later, so I didn't want to risk it."

"Oh, you smart man!" By now, the cat has hit her with his winning hug move and is being rewarded with an enthusiastic round of hugs and kisses from his new mommy. His loud purring sounds as though it rightfully belongs to a Sumatran tiger. "You wonderful man! Thank you! Thank you!"

"You're welcome, princess," I say, experiencing another one of those push–pull moments where something inside me swells and it's all I can do to keep it inside my body.

Anything for you.

I'd give you the earth just to keep you looking at me like that.

Please stick around in my life.

I lean in to receive her thank-you kiss. And get rewarded for my good deed with a possessive swat across my face from Mr. Ungrateful.

"Hey!" I tell the cat. "Remember who rescued your very little ass."

Naturally, this abuse makes Carly laugh. "He's got attitude. I *like* that. What's he called?"

"He's called whatever you name him."

"I shall call him…*Ruprecht*," she says, holding him up *Lion King* style and presenting him to the empty living room. Until he squirms, demanding to be released to explore his new home.

"Ruprecht. Oddly fitting," I say, pleased.

"Thank you, darling. You couldn't have got me a better gift."

"You're welcome."

"Did they give you some supplies for him?"

"Yeah. We're good for tonight." I check my watch. "And speaking of tonight, we'd better get going if we want to make our reservation."

"One second."

She closes her eyes and nuzzles her cheek against the cat's head, her smile lingering. It's one of those overflowing moments that has everything jammed inside it.

She's happy with her birthday present, which means I'm happy. We have a great night ahead of us. We're together. This, for me, is as good as my life is likely to get. I want to stay here, just like this, for as long as possible.

But her lids flick open, revealing a hint of vulnerability in those bright blue eyes as she opens her mouth. Hesitates.

"Do you think you could love me one day, Damon?" she asks quietly. "It would really make my life easier if you gave me a hint. One way or the other."

I freeze, classic deer in headlights as something unidentifiable inside me soars while my gut simultaneously plummets.

There it is. Another push–pull moment rising to make roadkill out of me when I least expect it.

And two answers battle for supremacy inside me. Neither winning. Neither losing.

I don't believe in love, Carly. Sorry.

I couldn't stop myself from loving you if I wanted to.

Too late, I realize that the moment has gone on way too long. That she's flushed with embarrassment now instead of flushed with excitement the way she was a minute ago. That I've ruined everything.

"It's okay," she says, hastily hitching her smile back into place as she avoids looking me in the face. She stands and sets the cat down. Heads for the bedroom as he scampers off. "Stupid question. Forget I said anything."

"Carly…"

"This crazy cat is peering out at me from under the bed. I'm guessing that's his new favorite hiding place." She tries to laugh, but the sound is strained. "I hope you've cat-proofed your entire apartment. Oh, and before I forget, Percy will be there at the opening tomorrow. Just wanted to give you a heads-up."

I freeze.

If there's *one* thing that can burst the thrilling bubble of the last few minutes, this announcement is it.

"Come again?"

"Percy. I thought the opening was a good chance to reach out and mend fences, so I invited him. I didn't expect him to come, but he says he'll be in town. I hope you don't mind."

In town my ass. I'd bet my entire portfolio that old Percy still wants her back. He probably received her invitation and dropped everything to be on the next flight back to her side.

The smart part of my brain, the portion that's helped me build a real estate empire, tells me to keep my mouth shut.

But the visceral, primitive part of me, the portion that seems determined to make me feel like shit tonight and to ruin things with Carly, seizes control and requires me to protect what's mine. What I *need*.

And that, sports fans, is Carly.

"I don't want you seeing him," I bark.

In my defense, I knew it was a fucking stupid thing to say even while the words were coming out of my mouth. The surest way to alienate someone is to march around issuing orders as though you can control the other person. But I'm discovering that jealousy and common sense cannot peacefully coexist inside me. Besides, it hasn't been that long since I faced down the legitimate fear that Carly might go back to him. I don't want to revisit that dark place.

Shit.

I really thought that guy was in our rearview mirror. Along with my uncertainties about whether Carly belongs with me or not.

That's what I get for being complacent.

Her brows go up, right on cue. She cocks her head.

"*What* did you just say?"

There it is. The lifeline fools like me need when we shoot off at the mouth. All I have to do is grab that lifeline. Back-pedal. Rephrase. Admit to an insecurity or two and politely request that she keep her contacts with the guy she almost married to a bare minimum. That's a much better plan. A strategic plan.

Too bad I ignore it.

I stare her in the face.

"I. Don't. Want. You. Seeing. Him."

Just like that, she weapons up, turns to ice and hits me with her crossed arms, dagger eyes and jagged tongue.

"Do American women respond to that? You booming out orders as though you're a bloody drill sergeant? Because *I* don't. And if I wanted a man to control my life, I'd run back home to Daddy."

"Why would you reach out to him? You want him back?"

"No, I don't want him back," she says, outraged. "Why are you behaving like this? Just because I'm in touch with an old friend?"

I don't like that phrasing. I don't like it at all.

"*In touch with?* What the fuck does *that* mean?"

She blinks, then quickly recovers her outrage. "He still texts me periodically. Just to say hello. I called to wish him happy Christmas. And that's the extent of it.

He lives in London, in case you forgot. It's not as though we could sneak around with each other, even if we wanted to. So I'd appreciate it if you stopped looking at me as though I've worked my way through all the men in the city."

"Why not mention it?"

"Because it's not that big a deal, you fool," she shouts. "It's not that big a deal to me and it shouldn't be that big a deal to you. Or maybe you haven't noticed that we're practically living together, and I can't wait to climb in bed with you every night?"

Not much could have pierced the red haze of my jealousy at that moment, but her sincerity seems to do the trick. It makes me pause, anyway. But there's something deeply unsettling about having those big blue eyes look at me with such glowing warmth one second, then realizing they've been hiding secrets about her ex the next. I don't know whether I'm seeing love or treachery. It puts me right back in that twisted place where I thought my mother was just my mother, only to discover that she was a liar, a cheat and a deserter. Three things I never would have suspected of her.

"Oh my God, Damon." She presses a hand to her chest, looking stricken. "What's gotten into you? You *know* how I feel about you."

That does it. I snap back into my right mind as though waking from some sort of altered state. And in that sudden moment of clarity, I catch a glimpse of how irrational I'm being.

Carly is not my mother.

She's nothing like my mother.

And I will not ruin her birthday with my creeping insanity.

"Sorry," I say, getting up and reaching for her, braced for her to smack my hand away. I'd deserve it if she did. But she's right there with me, opening her arms and pulling me in. We come together in a hard hug and sway back and forth while I try to recapture the joyous part of this evening. "Sorry. Sorry. *Sorry.*"

"Why did that make you so upset?"

"Because I don't like surprises. Or secrets." My voice is thick, so I pause to clear my throat. But that lump's not going anywhere. "And I've gotten used to having you around. I don't want anything to rock our boat."

A glimmer of exasperation appears in her expression as she pulls back. "Percy is incapable of rocking our boat. Take my word for it. But we don't need a repeat of the way you just behaved. I don't respond well to Neanderthals."

"Noted," I say wryly. Then I let her go. Swat her ass. "If we don't get a move on, you're going to have to deal with my hangry behavior. And no one wants that."

"We do not," she says grimly.

I laugh. "Get outta here."

She takes a few steps but pauses before she gets to the hallway, turning back.

"We don't have a problem, do we, Damon?"

My own uncertainty is enough to deal with. I can't handle hers, too. Much better to sweep it all under the rug and pretend it doesn't exist.

"Nah." I discover, too late, that it's impossible to look her in the face. I try to smile and realize I can't quite manage that, either. So I shove my hands in my pockets and hope I look convincingly unconcerned. "We're good."

"As long as we trust each other, right?" she asks lightly.

I nod, my mouth suddenly too dry to speak. Forcing myself to meet her gaze turns out to be a mistake, because those eyes ruin me. Her apparent honesty combines with my desperate desire to believe her, creating a compelling combination. But this whole Percy thing has put a crack in something that was fine an hour ago. I want to believe her, but now there's a shadow over my heart.

Correction: now there's a shadow over the crater where my heart used to be. And I can't stop myself from thinking poisonous thoughts.

You're not going to stand there using those eyes as a weapon against me, Carly. I won't let you yank my guts out.

17

CARLY

"DID YOU JUST SELL ANOTHER PAINTING?" Michele asks in a shocked whisper at my show the following night. "You're not going to have any inventory left to sell online. And we're going to have to send you home in an armored car tonight with all your new coins and Benjamins."

We enjoy one of our girlish conspiratorial giggles together, although I like to think we're much more sophisticated than the college freshman we used to be, whispering about the handsome guys we passed as we walked to classes. For tonight's launch of my soon-to-be art empire, we both wear sexy little black dresses with heels. We've both enjoyed a healthy serving of champagne. And we both know how hard I've worked for this moment and how much it means to me and my career hopes.

"I did sell another painting!"

"Which one?"

"*Existential Threat*," I say, pointing to the large painting that consists mainly of angry slashes and swoops in every dark color in my arsenal. Basically a scream on canvas. As she well knows, I began the painting my junior year, after a particularly nasty disagreement with my father, who wondered why I kept resisting his efforts to get me to transfer to Oxford to finish school. "Who would have ever thought that my emotional turmoil would bring me such a pretty penny all these years later?"

"I know, right?" She sips her champagne, gazing thoughtfully at the canvas. "And, no offense, but what kind of person wants to stare at that all day? It's like the one piece of artwork guaranteed to make you hide in bed all day if you stare at it too long."

"I don't ask questions," I say, laughing. "I just accept checks."

"Have you broken six figures yet tonight?"

"Just did," I say triumphantly, unable to believe my enormous good fortune or that I might possibly be able to make a career out of something I love as much as I love painting.

"Cheers to that."

We toast each other. Sip while the well-dressed and well-connected crowd of art lovers mills around us and studies my work. One woman makes a face and backs away from one of my precious babies as though the thing has offended her. Just like that, all my simmering anxieties rise to the surface and cause me to question whether I can earn a living this way.

"I hate this," I say, rubbing my roiling belly. "It's like watching a teacher grade my paper and give me failing marks."

"You want to be an artist? You've got big dreams? Well, suck it up like the rest of us."

"Thank you for that utter lack of sympathy," I say, shooting her a glare.

"So how are things going with Damon?" She discreetly tips her head at where he's standing near the bar with his brothers. "He's looking stupid handsome tonight in his dark suit and dark shirt, I must say. Why wear a tie when you can pull off the George Clooney look?"

As though he feels the weight of our attention, Damon looks in my direction and gives me a slow once-over that culminates in a sexy bite of his lip that tells me exactly what he's thinking and what he plans to do with me later, all of it X-rated. Naturally, I blush as I try to smother my responsive grin.

Naturally, Michele notices.

"You're in love with him," she says.

I keep sipping and say nothing. I don't dare risk it. By now my face is positively alight. I can only be grateful that the ensuing inferno won't ruin my paintings, which are in water-based acrylics.

"I knew it!" she says with unmitigated glee. "You *are*!"

"Is now the time for this intensely personal conversation?" I ask, trying to maintain *some* dignity.

"Yes! So is he in love with you? Has he told you yet?"

"No," I say glumly. "I'm starting to think he's allergic to love. And it doesn't help that we had a huge fight last night."

"About what?"

I hesitate, knowing what's coming. "Percy."

"I *knew* it." She scowls in the general direction of the appetizer table, where Percy and my father are engaged in deep conversation. "I don't know why you had to invite him. Stubborn redhead. Maybe one of these days you'll start listening to me."

"Like I've told you a million times, I want to mend bridges with him. I can't stand the idea of him hating me. We've been friends our whole lives." I hesitate. "Plus, I never actually thought he'd come."

"Yeah, well, I'd love to see how understanding *you'd* feel if Damon rolled up with some beautiful and wealthy ex-fiancée and started talking about renewing his *friend-ship* with her."

"Percy and I were engaged for about ten minutes," I say hotly. God knows I have no other leg to stand on here. I shudder to think what sort of rampaging Godzilla I'd turn into if I thought I had competition for Damon's affection. I can't get him to tell me he loves me as it is. And if another woman entered the picture…?

"*That's* your defense?"

"Oh, whatever," I snap. "The bigger issue is Damon's jealousy and my bad reaction to it. He acted very controlling. Very alpha."

"I'm sure you don't complain about how alpha he is in bed," she says, her brows creeping higher.

Since this is perfectly true, I decide to ignore it.

"You want me to listen to you? This is your time to give me some good advice before Damon and I ruin our relationship over nonsense. Don't blow it," I tell her.

"Fine. Is Damon truly controlling? Because, I gotta tell you, that's not the vibe I've ever gotten from him. Which makes me think he's insecure. You need to get to the bottom of that."

This has the ring of good common sense. Which is one of the reasons I keep Michele around.

"Speak of the devil," she says before I can answer, her voice dropping. "Here comes Percy. You might not want to look *too* happy to see him. I'm out."

"What?" I say with a vague note of alarm. I greeted Percy earlier when he first arrived, but I'm not sure I'm ready to have any sort of substantive conversation with him under Damon's watchful eye. "You just going to *leave* me?"

"You'll be fine," she says blithely as she sails off. "And if I spend any more time with him tonight, I'm going to fall asleep standing up."

I'd love to read her the riot act, but there's no time. Percy arrives looking cautious. Hopeful.

I decide to just plunge in. Get it over with.

"I'm so glad you came," I tell him, excruciatingly aware of Damon's hard stare from across the room. I feel as though I'm being watched by Sauron's evil eye from all the *Lord of the Rings* movies. To make matters worse, my father also hovers on the periphery, no doubt hoping I'll be able to snatch a few thousand-dollar bills from Percy's deep pockets before the conversation is over. "It means the world to me."

"And me," he says, his expression brightening. "Didn't feel right for us to not talk."

"I agree." I take a closer look at him, noting his sparkling eyes and something else that seems new about him. It's not his clothes or hair. But there's something unidentifiable about him that makes him seem more... energetic. Alive. "You look great, by the way. How are things at home?"

This is evidently the cue he's been waiting for. He breaks into a wide grin, all sunshine and hearts, and suddenly I know.

"Percy, you've met someone," I cry, delighted.

"I've met someone," he says, laughing as his face floods with color. "And she's been under my nose this whole time. She's the large-animal veterinarian in the village. Loves nothing better than mucking about in the stables and taking long hikes with me. She's not a redhead like you, sadly, but I plan to keep her around indefinitely."

"See?" I can hardly contain my excitement. He deserves the absolute best. Truly. He's always been such a class act. "What did I tell you? Why would you want *me* hanging around when you have someone like *that*? You'd better marry her, Percy. She sounds like your soul mate."

"That's the plan. In good time. If she'll have me."

"I'm sure she will."

"She pushed me to come tonight, to be honest," he says, leaning in and switching to a conspiratorial tone. "Wanted me to see you. Make sure I'm completely over you. No offense."

"None taken," I say dryly. "Glad to be of service."

"Anyway…" He ducks his head. Tugs an earlobe. "I just wanted to tell you. And to let you know I expect you to come round for dinner the next time you're home."

"That's a date."

We beam at each other for a wonderful second and it feels like old times, only a million times better. And a moment like that can only conclude with a hug and kiss.

We pull each other in for a tight squeeze that puts the final few nails in our mended fences.

"Give her all my best wishes," I tell him, squeezing his forearms when we pull apart.

"And you have mine," he says with a trace of melancholy as he glances in Damon's direction (Damon is still watching us but, to his credit, he seems bemused now rather than murderous) before heading off again. "I'll see you in a bit."

I'm still watching Percy go and breathing a huge sigh of relief when my father immediately swoops in. I suppose I should give him credit for waiting until the conversation is over and not pulling up a chair to watch the proceedings with a bowl of popcorn.

"Oh, for God's sake, Daddy," I say, grimacing. "You should look up *subtlety* in the dictionary one of these days. Familiarize yourself with the word."

"No time for that." He takes my arm and steers me behind one of the partial walls in the middle of the room that features one of my paintings on each side, where we can have a bit more privacy. "What was that all about with Percy just now? Looked very cozy."

"It was a pleasant conversation between old friends," I say flatly, determined to shut down any hopes of a fantasy reconciliation between me and Percy that he might be harboring. "That's all. Nothing to get excited about. He's actually met someone else. Seems happy."

"To no one's surprise, Charlotte," he says, looking as though someone has been bludgeoned right in front of him. "Of course someone would snatch him up. What did you think would happen when you foolishly cut him loose?"

"I really can't deal with this tonight," I say, rolling my eyes. "I have paintings to sell. If there's nothing else...?"

"Luckily, Damon Black still seems very smitten with you. I've been watching him watch you all night. I don't suppose you've closed *that* deal yet, have you?"

My heart doesn't sink so much as it plummets

through the floor. I'm surprised at my visceral reaction to the mere suggestion of me marrying Damon, but there's no ignoring the sharp yearning I feel inside. Which, by the way, bears no resemblance to the vague feeling of dread I always experienced when I suspected Percy might propose. The mere thought of living the rest of my life accompanied by Damon's smile and laughter, his humor, strength, smarts and sexiness is enough to make me float away like the helium balloon-powered house in that movie *Up*. And the idea of having *children* with Damon? I have to tiptoe up on it and give my heart time to adjust. Otherwise, it will burst from happiness.

Any woman would be lucky to spend her life with Damon. I could only pray to be so lucky.

"My personal life is none of your concern," I tell my father, threading my voice with liberal amounts of barbed wire and jagged glass in the hopes that he drops the subject.

It doesn't work, though. It never does with him.

"So no proposals, then," he says as he rubs his chin, speaking to himself as much as to me. "Well, it's still early days yet."

That's a valid point. I try to take heart. Damon and I have only been together for about seven months. Some men take longer to give their whole hearts. Hopefully, Damon falls into that category. As opposed to the *it's not you, it's me* or the *I doubt I'll ever get married* categories. Given his horrendous family history? It's entirely possible that marriage isn't on his radar. Anyone whose parents went through a terrible divorce is likely to be gun-shy.

"But you *would* marry Damon if he asked you," my father says.

"Of course I would," I say indignantly, the champagne having loosened my tongue enough to make this little slip. "What fool wouldn't?"

"Well, as I said," my father says, shrugging. "One billionaire is as good as any other."

Unbelievable. As per usual, my happiness is a secondary consideration to my father. If that.

"Could you *please* stop being so crass and shallow?"

He tries to act surprised and wounded. "What? I'm trying to say that he'd be a welcome addition to the family. You can't blame a man for that. He certainly helped me out of a large financial jam when he purchased my paintings at a generous price. *That* was welcome."

With that, I hit my limit of my father.

"Right, then," I snap. "This conversation is over."

I start to walk around the half wall so that I can rejoin the party.

And nearly run directly into Damon.

Sudden paralytic shock freezes me into place, which is a good thing, because he's holding three flutes of champagne that he evidently meant to share with me and my father. For one arrested second I wonder how much he just heard or if he heard anything at all, but the shifting expression on his face solves that puzzle for me.

Disbelief… Confusion… Hurt… Cold fury.

"Damon," I say helplessly.

I wouldn't think that the moment could get any worse, but my father stiffens upon hearing Damon's name and manages to look conspicuously guilty, like a toddler swearing he didn't eat a pre-dinner cookie even though he has chocolate smeared all over his mouth.

"I don't know if you caught any of that, Damon," he says with what he clearly hopes is a winning chuckle, "but I hope there's no misunderstanding. What we meant to say is—"

Jesus Christ. As if I'd risk letting my father clarify things for me.

"*I* will speak to Damon," I tell my father coldly. "You've done enough for the night."

My father pauses. Slowly turns to go.

A nasty smile inches its way across Damon's face. A crooked smile. A soulless smile.

"Why rush off?" He hands a flute to my father, then one to me. I numbly take it. "I thought we should toast to Carly's success tonight. She's got everyone eating out of her hand. Well, she already had me and Percy eating out of her hand, but now she's got everyone else, too."

I stiffen.

"To Princess Carly," he says, raising his glass. "Skilled painter and bewitcher of true billionaires like Percy and wannabe billionaires like me. Long may she reign."

I flinch as he downs his champagne, puts the empty glass on a nearby tray and, lobbing a final glare in my direction, stalks off, taking all the room's air with him.

The sight of him walking off—possibly walking out of my life—jars me into action.

"If you ruin things for me, I'll never forgive you, Daddy," I furiously whisper at my father, then take off after Damon.

I HURRY AFTER DAMON, propelled by a sense of urgency bordering on panic and struck by an overwhelming sense of déjà vu. Another party. Me following him down another deserted hallway. Another high-stakes conversation to follow. Only this time I feel as though my entire life is on the line. Probably because it is.

"Please don't make me chase after you," I call after him, teetering in my heels as I try to keep up with his long strides. "We need to talk."

"This isn't the time," he says, turning into a small lounge area where we left our coats when we arrived at the gallery earlier. The end table lamp throws harsh shadows across his face, making him look even more forbidding. "Go enjoy your success. You don't need me around for that."

"Of course I need you around for that."

"I don't want to ruin your big night for you. Let's do this later."

"This is far more important. There's no way I can enjoy myself when I've hurt your feelings and I didn't mean to," I say, shutting the door behind me. "We need to get this straightened out."

"Not much to straighten, princess." A muscle flexes in his jaw. He finds his coat on the rack and slides his arms into it, his movements choppy. Slings his scarf around his neck. A better option than using it to strangle me, which he would probably love to do. "I think we're pretty straight."

"No, we're not," I say, sidestepping to block him when he heads for the door again. "I know what you think you heard—"

"Correction: what I heard."

"—and I admit my father wouldn't care if I married a ninety-five-year-old man on death's door as long as he was a billionaire. But that's not me."

"Sure sounded like you." He meets my gaze for the first time, forcing me to recoil. There's so much hurt and anger in his flashing brown eyes. So much reproach in his face and quiet voice, even though it's rough with emotion. I'd almost prefer that he yell at me. Smash that lamp. Anything other than this deathly stillness. "I'm almost positive I recognized your voice when you said you'd be a fool not to marry a billionaire. I'm guessing that's why you brought Percy back tonight, right, princess? It's always healthy to play both ends against the middle. Spark a little competition between potential rich husbands. I'm sure your father's taught you that."

"No," I say, frustration making my voice pitch higher. "I keep telling you. I don't want Percy. I could've already married him by now if he's what I wanted. We just exchanged pleasantries and wished each other well. That's it. You saw our whole conversation. He even told

me he's met someone else. He seems excited about her. And I'm excited for him."

For one arrested second, this information seems to interest him. His vague frown of consternation makes me wonder if I've broken through some of his pain to reach the man underneath this forbidding figure in his dark suit and topcoat. But then his lips tighten into a sneer and I know it won't be that easy. It could never be that easy with Damon Black.

"Touching. By the way, before this conversation goes any further, you should know that my deal fell through. Seven months wasted on my pipe dream. So I'm not a billionaire after all."

"*So?*" The non sequitur throws me for a loop. "I mean, I'm sorry you're disappointed, but who cares?"

"You and your father, clearly. I thought you should know. It might figure into your grand scheme."

"There's no grand scheme and I don't give a damn about your net worth. I'm busy working on my own. Which you might have noticed tonight if you weren't so busy being angry at the world."

We stare at each other in a poisonous silence. I'm desperate to clear up this misunderstanding, but I'm terrified to open my mouth and somehow make things worse. I'm not doing very well at following his train of thought at the moment.

"Fascinating," he finally says. "So what was all that about your big plan to marry a billionaire?"

"Not some random billionaire, you blind idiot," I shout, knowing it's a bad idea to lose my temper and pour gasoline on this raging fire. But I can't help myself. Long weeks and months of pretending I only feel so much for him and no more have already worn down my reserves of self-control. Honestly, it's a relief to open the taps and let it all gush out. "*You!* I'd have to be a fool not to marry *you*!"

Something shifts in his expression, wiping out all the turbulence and leaving what looks like bland curiosity. The kind you might see when a stranger on the street asks you the time.

But I know him well enough to see the intensity burning in his eyes. There's no mistaking it.

Damon's not indifferent to what I just said. Far from it. He's all but holding his breath in his eagerness to learn more.

Even so, he hangs on to his stubborn pride and bravado like James Bond dangling over the ledge of the fiftieth floor of some skyscraper and holding on by his fingertips. He hikes up his chin and hits me with a hateful little hitch of his shoulders that passes as a shrug.

"I'm having a tough time keeping up, princess. I'm not a blue blood. Not a billionaire. You understand my confusion."

"Well, let me clear it up for you." I get in his face, my curled fingers itching to smack the nasty smirk off his face. It's bad enough when the woman says the L-word first and risks driving the man off, screaming, never to be seen again. Worse for me to hurl the news at him like this, in anger, but what choice is there? I can't let this wound fester and ruin our relationship. I'll do anything to keep that from happening. Even swallow my pride and face my biggest fear. "I'd have to be a fool not to marry you because I'm in love with you. At moments like this, it gets hard to remember exactly *why* I'm in love with you, but I am. I don't care what color your blood is. Couldn't care less about your zeros or lack thereof."

He says nothing, but I detect a small tremor in his chin. A slight chink in his armor. That's all the encouragement I need. Now that I've opened the door, the words can't fly out of my mouth fast enough.

And even though he's never mentioned words like *love*, *marriage* or *children*, I suddenly can't wait to share my feelings with him. He's worth the risk. I know he is.

"Damon—"

He clears his throat. "Let's finish this later."

That's when it hits me that he's more scared than I am. That's a good sign, isn't it?

"No," I say. "You need to hear this right now."

"Carly—"

"The only thing I care about is that I feel like I'm glowing when I'm with you." I feel myself lighting up even as I say it. That's what he does to me. "Like I could do anything as long as you're in my life. Even my hair comes alive when you're in the room. I know that sounds sappy and stupid, but that's how I feel. And it seems like you would've noticed that in the last seven months. Or maybe when I gave you that heart painting yesterday and called it *Joie*. Maybe I should've called it *Love* instead. Maybe *that* would've broken through your thick skull. But you're too busy trying to make sure that I'm not your mother and trying to make sure that you're not your father to see what's right in front of you. I'm *here*. I *love you*."

With that, he abruptly looks away. Roughly wipes each eye with the heel of his hand.

"You want my money. Your father needs my money," he says stubbornly. "Don't pretend he doesn't."

"I'm not pretending anything! What money have you given *me*? I've done all this on my own," I say, flapping a hand toward the party and all of my paintings. "You offered to help, but I did it myself. And now I get accused of wanting you for your money?"

"Your father—"

"Don't mix me up with my father. *He's* having hard times. *He's* a gold digger. I don't deny it. I admit it. But he's a grown man. He can take care of himself. Hell, I've told him that *he* should marry rich, since money's such an issue. And I told *you* that you didn't have to make that deal with him if you didn't want to. But *you* decided—"

"I did it for *you!*" he roars, all that emotion surging through his aloof façade like a tsunami riding a tornado. It's a wonder I don't tumble over backward with the force of it. "You think I needed his fucking paintings? I don't even collect Baroque pieces! I did it for *you!*"

"*Why* did you do it?"

"Because I want you and your family to have what you need!"

"*Why?*"

"Because I'd do anything for *you!* Don't you get it? Haven't *you* been paying attention?"

This man is going to rip my heart out.

"Because you love me." I hurry forward to put my hands on either side of his hard, beloved face. He's boiling hot and rigid as one of my father's marble busts, all his emotions bubbling over into his reddened cheeks. He tries to back up and twist away, but I follow him. Cup his downturned face again. Hang on when he stiffens even further. "That's all you ever have to do, Damon. Love me. That's all I want. And that's between *you* and *me*. Not you, me and my father. Or you, me and your money. It will *never* have anything to do with money. No matter what lies you tell yourself."

He hesitates, bowing his head and reaching up to hold one of my wrists.

Just the opening I need.

"Okay?" I run my thumbs over his cheekbones. Slowly bring him down, so my mouth can reach him. I give him a lingering kiss that sparks a fire as he clings to me. I kiss him again, harder. I rejoice when he takes over with a masculine growl of intent, possessing my mouth with an all-consuming urgency that will leave my lips swollen later. But I break free before I wind up flat on my back over on the sofa, opening my legs to receive him. Not because that's not what I want. But because I'm desperate to make sure he believes me. And I won't even worry about that fact that he's just heard all about my love for him but hasn't used the L-word himself. That's a struggle for another day. For now? I need to make sure he's around another day. I stare up at him, unwilling to break eye contact. I may well lose him if I do. "*Okay? You have to believe me. You know I love you, Damon.*"

He stares back, emotions scrolling through his expression. All the emotions. Banked joy. Poorly controlled fear. Hope. Despair. Confusion. I see it all. I *feel* it all. I know he wants to believe me. And I know, suddenly and sickeningly, that he'll never allow himself to believe me. Just like I know that this battle was lost before I ever laid eyes on him that night at Bemelmans.

Suddenly it's over. He pulls my hands down and steps back, breaking the physical contact between us with the finality of a door slamming in my face. Leaving me standing there on what should be the greatest night of my life, reeling.

I watch, disbelieving, as his expression reverts to utter blankness dotted with soulless shark eyes. Only the sound of his ragged breathing lets me know I didn't just imagine his kiss.

"Here's the thing, princess," he says quietly. "When your mother walks out on you? She takes most of the things you know with her. And you don't trust the rest."

I hesitate, letting that sink in. I want to make sure I fully understand his point before I let him have it.

Don't think I'm a monster. I get what he's saying. Honestly, I do. But I am *so* sick of his invisible mother and her horrible claw marks all over this man. I'm so sick of her keeping him from me and him refusing to fight the good fight. He doesn't have to let his past ruin our future.

If only he would make that choice.

"Here's the thing, Damon," I say, squaring my shoulders. "You're the smartest man I know. Smart enough to know that I'm the absolute best thing that's ever happened to you. Smart enough not to let your insecurities drive me away. And *I'm* smart enough to give you some time to see if you can get past your bullshit. There's going to come a moment, probably sooner rather than later, when you start to miss me and your fear of losing me is a million time worse than your fear of admitting you love me. So if and when you get your act together, I'll be waiting for my abject apology. And I mean *abject*. You know where to find me. Just don't take too long. I only have so much patience."

I turn and walk out, wiping the lipstick off my mouth so I can return to my party, and let the door bang shut on his stricken expression.

19

DAMON

IT TURNS out that frenzied workouts and/or jogging laps around the better part of Central Park don't burn enough energy to clear Carly out of my mind. Not even for two consecutive seconds. Other things that don't work, in no particular order? Drinking. Working. Reading. Watching TV. Staring at ceilings or walls. Sleeping.

She's there. She's always there.

And yet she's not *here*, goddammit.

Evidently, I've lost all ability to function without her. The only thing left is misery. By Thursday, I'm so sick of myself, my churning thoughts and my sulking that it's all I can do to look at my reflection in the mirror after my shower.

Swear to God, I hate that guy. I want to punch him in his stupid fucking face.

Under normal circumstances, the idea of skipping a day of work strikes me as inconceivable. Without my epic and indispensable presence, the New York real estate market—hell, let's call it the global real estate market—will immediately collapse, turn to dust and blow away on a stiff breeze, sending economies everywhere into a major depression. You'd think so, anyway, based on my lifelong work ethic.

But now? Fuck work. Fuck the office. Fuck everything.

"Enjoy yourself," my executive assistant says when I call to tell her that I'm going to the Hamptons and therefore won't be in the office today. "You've earned it."

But there's no mistaking the relief in her tone when she hears that I won't be blessing her with my sparkling personality today.

So I hit the road and head out to my family home, thinking that the long drive to the beach may help clear my head. Unfortunately, it turns out that long drives to the beach belong on my list of things that don't help clear my head.

I'm in love with you, Damon.

I get there by late morning and tell the startled staff to ignore me. Settle in the library, where my new Baroque paintings don't exactly blend with the Picasso sketches. Make myself a couple of dirty martinis and wonder whether my ability to ruin my own life is a talent other people share or my own unique gift. I'm giving some serious thought to skipping the glass on the next few rounds and just drinking straight from the pitcher when I hear unwelcome footsteps and voices in the hallway.

"He's probably in here." The door swings open and Griffin's head appears. He surveys the scene, spotting me on the sofa. "Yeah, he's in here."

Before I have time to react, he and Ryker come inside and hit me with twin pallbearer faces.

"Fuck," I say, welcoming this intrusion the way five-star hotels welcome bedbug infestations.

"Nice to see you too," Ryker says. "We came to cheer you up, dickhead."

"No, we didn't," Griffin says, scowling. "This is an intervention. I don't do *cheer*. I wouldn't have dragged my ass all the way out here on a weekday for *cheer*."

"Is that important?" Ryker says, giving him a look.

"I'm here to tell him to get his act together and stop fucking up at the office." Griffin goes to the drink cabinet, pours a bourbon, passes it to Ryker and starts to work on a gin and tonic for himself. "His personal life is his own business. If he wants to be miserable during non-work hours, that's his right as an American. It's in the Constitution."

"Yeah, but—" Ryker begins.

"Look," I say wearily when this shows every sign of continuing indefinitely. "I don't care what you're calling it. I don't need it. I'm fine. It's all under control. Thanks for stopping by. See you back in the city."

"You're not fine. You look like shit," Ryker says as they sit on either side of me.

"Okay, well, I'm fine with looking like shit," I say, then down the rest of my dirty martini and start to get up for a refill.

Without a word, Griffin snatches my glass and shoves me back down. "Let's not," he says. "You don't need anything else. I'm already getting a contact high from the fumes wafting off you. Let's just get this whole awkward conversation over with so we can move on with our lives."

I know, from painful experience, that these two clowns can be as stubborn as a Taurus mule, especially when they put their heads together about something. Plus, I can tell by the grim determination on Griffin's face that a scuffle, if not an outright brawl, is in my immediate future if my ass doesn't remain in contact with the sofa cushion for the duration. Since I'm in the middle of a pleasant buzz and don't have the energy required to win this round if it comes to blows, I decide to ride it out. The sooner they say their piece, the sooner they'll leave me in peace. I hope.

"Fine," I say, resting my elbows on my knees and bracing myself. "Let's hear it."

Griffin opens his mouth—

"I'll handle this," Ryker says quickly, shooting him a warning look. "The last thing we need is for you to make this worse with your abrasive personality."

"Suit yourself, Ry," Griffin says, then makes a show of getting comfortable by leaning back, crossing his legs and taking a leisurely sip of his drink. "Just don't fuck it up."

"You've got to get Carly back," Ryker tells me, shooting Griffin a final sidelong glare. "You can't go down in flames like this."

"Sure I can," I say, incredulous. Who among us can be surprised that I've screwed things up with Carly? I don't exactly have a long history of successful relationships under my belt. "Have we met?"

"We're trying to help you not be your own worst enemy," Ryker says, making zero effort to hide his exasperation. "Stop being such a hardass all the time."

Griffin frowns. "I thought *I* was the hardass in the family."

"You're the ass*hole*," Ryker tells him. "There's a difference."

"True," Griffin says, his expression clearing.

"Anyway, Damon, what's the issue?" Ryker says. "We're here. Maybe you need to bounce some ideas off us."

He waits patiently.

Griffin, meanwhile, pulls out his phone with his free hand and scrolls through emails.

I scowl. *This* is what my life has come to. It's my own fault for getting myself into the pathetic position of receiving romantic advice from Bill and Ted here. Having not learned my lesson the last time I confided in one of these two morons, I mentioned the other day, in passing, that Carly and I had hit a rough patch. Now *this*.

Although, come to think of it, they're both happy in their new relationships. To my knowledge, neither one of them is spending his long and lonely nights alone with only his blue balls to keep him company. Maybe, if I confide a bit more about my situation, one or the other of them might stumble onto an encouraging word of wisdom. It's worth a shot. I can hardly be worse off than I am now.

I clear my throat.

"Carly, ah, loves me. She says she's in love with me."

"So, naturally, you've lost the will to live and look like shit," Griffin says, still scrolling.

That's why he's the family asshole.

In a sign of how close my emotions are to the surface these days, that's all it takes for me to lose my shit. I surge to my feet and bend down to get in his face.

"You want a go at me?" I roar. Rather than respond, Griffin yawns and taps out a message on his phone. This, naturally, throws ten gallons of gasoline on the situation. I shove his shoulders. Griffin raises a hand to ward me off. "Huh? You think *this* is the time for your —"

"Sit your ass down." Ryker materializes between us, puts his hands on my shoulders and backs me up a couple of steps until I jerk away to fume nonviolently. We've been through this drill before, unfortunately. With Griffin around, you always need a person on standby in case someone lunges for his throat. "Focus. What's the problem with Carly? You've got your eye on someone else? You've found someone better?"

"What?" I say, flopping onto the nearest chair. The idea is so patently absurd that I can't hide my incredulity. There's no one better than Carly. Never has been, never will be. *"No.* Of course not."

"She's moving too fast for you?" Ryker continues.

I think about how I gave her the key to my apartment almost immediately. Then I think about how I just happened to wander into the engagement ring section at Harry Winston the other day.

"No."

"Well, what?" Ryker asks blankly.

I shrug, struggling to put the other night's ugly scene into words. I still can't quite figure out how things went sideways on us so quickly.

"She, ah, invited her ex-fiancé to her show the other night."

"Ah." Griffin looks up from his phone, nodding sagely. "So she fucked him."

A haze of red descends on my vision at this point, so I'm not exactly sure what happens next. All I know is that my fingertips are mere *inches* from Griffin's throat this time before Ryker intervenes again. He calmly hauls me back, snarling, and shoves me back into the chair. Then he turns to Griffin.

"For *once*," Ryker says tiredly.

"Sorry," Griffin says, tapping on his phone again.

Ryker sits on the coffee table in front of me, blocking my view of the asshole. "Right here," he says, gesturing at his eyes. "Ignore him. Focus on me. What's the problem? You think she's getting back with the other guy?"

"*No,*" I say, and I don't. Not really. Not when I'm in my right frame of mind. I've seen how she looks at me. I know how she responds to me when I touch her. I know what we've built together these last months. But I also know that there's no telling what I might drive her to if I can't get a grip on the insidious voice in my head that keeps telling me that she'll leave me one day. If not for Percy, then for some other valid reason. Because I'm a fucking loser and the clock is running on when she'll discover that inescapable fact. "But he's part of her world. He's got more money than we do. And her father just wants her to marry someone with money. He doesn't give a fuck whether it's me or the other guy."

Ryker blinks. Frowns. "And she wants…?"

"Me," I say.

Ryker's frown deepens. "And this is a problem because…?"

I open my mouth, struggling to describe the brick wall that materializes in my face every time I think about next steps with Carly, but Griffin beats me to the punch.

"It's classic Damon," he says, lowering his phone. "Classic Type A control-freak behavior. Classic oldest child of divorce behavior. That's why he's so arrogant. It's a defense mechanism because he knows he'll never be good enough in his own mind."

"What?" Ryker and I both say, glancing around at him.

"Damon thinks he's got to be perfect," Griffin continues blithely. "Think about it. Perfect student. The perfect son to sweep in and help Dad save the business. The perfect workaholic to sweep in and make the business bigger and better than it's ever been. The perfect guy to sweep in and help us break the billion-dollar mark. He's got to work his fingers to the bone or die trying to be perfect. Why? Because if he'd been perfect back in the day, like he thinks he should have, Mom would never have walked out on the family."

I freeze, stunned into paralysis.

"That's what a ten-year-old thinks, right, Damon? She never would've picked some other guy over Dad. The richer guy over Dad right when it looked like Dad's business was about to go belly up. How am I doing, Damon? And now it's in the back of your mind that Carly will walk out if you're not perfect. Why bother letting her in if she's only going to walk out? Just keep that door slammed in her face. Am I getting close?"

I gape at him. Not because I haven't had these same half-baked ideas floating around in my brain, because I have. But because these self-destructive thoughts sound so absurd when spoken aloud by someone else. And because I never would have suspected that *Griffin*, of all people, possesses this sort of insight.

"Here's the thing, Damon," Griffin says, nailing me with that penetrating look of his. "I'm *pretty* sure she's already noticed that you're not perfect."

I'm in love with you. At moments like this, it gets hard to remember exactly why I'm in love with you, but I am.

I wince, fighting the sensation that Griffin has

clamped defibrillator paddles on either side of my head and shocked some sense into me. Could he be right? Is that all there is to my insanity? Just…*insecurity*? Just standard, garden-variety irrational fear? And if that's my entire problem, am I stupid enough to let it stand between me and Carly?

No. No, I am not. I may be exceptionally stupid at times. But I'm not *that* stupid.

There's going to come a moment, probably sooner rather than later, when you start to miss me and your fear of losing me is a million times worse than your fear of admitting you love me.

Jesus. What have I been doing? Pushing Carly away?

What the actual fuck have I been doing?

I'm still sitting there with revelations reverberating through me when Griffin kills the rest of his drink, sets the glass down on the coffee table, gives a single decisive clap and stands.

"Let's go," he barks at Ryker, who looks startled. "Our work here is done. You're driving."

"But…" Ryker says, sadly eyeballing the rest of his drink. "We just got here."

"Yeah, but I've got stuff to do back at the office," Griffin tells him. "Besides. He gets it."

"I *don't* get it." I stand too, oddly reluctant to let my unlikely cavalry right off and leave me alone with my churning thoughts. I feel encouraged, yeah, but there's still plenty of room for me to screw this whole thing up once they leave me to my own devices. "You two had the exact same fucked-up childhood that I did. Mom walked out on you two just like she walked out on me. Why aren't *you* screwed up?"

"We are," Griffin gravely assures me. "We're just screwed up in slightly different ways."

Well, *that's* certainly true, I decide with a bark of laughter. Especially in Griffin's case.

"Yeah, but how do you keep that from torching your relationships?" I think about how happy these two have been since that eventful night at Bemelmans last year when we all met our matches. Every day is Christmas now for these two, judging by the looks on their faces most of the time. "Why do you make it look so easy? What do you know that I don't know?"

To my surprise, Griffin clamps his hands on either side of my face and gives me a look of purest empathy. No mischief for once. Just brotherly support and under-standing.

"Nothing. We figured it out. You will too." He gives my cheeks a stinging smack. "As soon as you grow a pair of real balls."

"Fucking asshole," I mutter, laughing and energized as I watch them wave goodbye and file out.

Time for me to get my princess back. And to seal this deal. For once and for all.

SHE GLIDES in like the queen of everything without bothering to notice the fancy Friday night crowd here at Bemelmans. Forget about making eye contact with anyone or acknowledging the pianist plinking away on the grand. The server gets a nod of thanks as he seats her at the leather banquette against the wall at one of the small round tables nearest where I sit. A hint of a dimpled smile as she accepts the menu. Then the server walks off and she lowers her eyes to study the drink selections, retreating into a cool bubble of aloofness that only the brave would dare try to penetrate.

Too bad I'm not feeling that brave at the moment. Hard to feel brave when the only thing standing between you and a miserable and lonely existence is your questionable ability to explain your inexplicable behavior. If only I could press a button on my phone and receive instant assistance from SEAL Team Six. God knows I could use the backup.

But this is a good first step, right? She agreed to meet me for drinks. Actually showed up. She's wearing the same bun and dress from the night we met, significant details that are not lost on me.

I breathe a little easier.

I watch her and wonder how to get myself over there to where she is. The distance is less than ten feet, but it may as well be the other side of the Grand Canyon. Not to mention the fact that my wonky nerves and tight throat give me a less than fifty percent chance of saying anything coherent when I get there.

But then something miraculous happens.

She looks up from her menu, makes eye contact and gives me a hint of a smile. Not the whole thing, mind you, but enough to encourage and energize me into standing, downing the rest of my dirty martini and heading over.

A woman like Carly deserves a brave man.

I can pretend to be that man. With her by my side? I can pretend for the rest of my life.

"Hey," I say, clearing the frog from my throat. "Mind if I join you?"

She gives me a chilly once-over and reverts to studying her menu as though it contains instructions on how to defuse the ticking bomb strapped to her chair.

"I couldn't say. Are you here to break off another little piece of my heart? Because if you are, you can fuck off right now."

Her challenge thus issued, she nails me with that blue-eyed gaze, which is hard and uncompromising now. I could almost laugh if I weren't on the verge of shitting my pants. I knew she'd have some hoops for me to jump through. I should've also expected them to be roughly ten feet high and only two feet around.

"Your heart's very important to me. I plan to take good care of it," I say.

"Hmm. You wouldn't know it."

The server makes an appearance. "What can I get you?"

"Dirty martini," she says, defrosting for the man.

"And for you, sir?"

"Same. Thanks."

The server walks off. Like magic, a layer of ice re-encases Carly's entire body. She stares at me, waiting with her brows raised.

You know what? Fuck this scared routine. I'm a grown man. Past time to act like it.

I sit down, on her left, crowding her on the banquette. She stiffens and tries to shift away, but I'm not having it.

We've—*I've*—wasted enough time.

So I wrap my right arm around her waist. Settle her exactly where she is.

"You don't get to just show up and touch me and have everything be perfectly fine again," she says, her voice thick now. A little wobbly. "It doesn't work like that."

"I know it doesn't," I say, then kiss her bare shoulder and shudder with the relief of immersing myself in her lavender scent again. "But I'm hoping you can listen to music with me until my drink gets here. I need some liquid courage to tell you a few things you should know."

"You're not going to make me cry," she says, hastily wiping her eyes with her index finger, mindful of her makeup. "Just so you know."

"Shh." I kiss her shoulder again and feel some of the

tension leave her body. "I don't want to make you cry. I just want to make sure you understand me."

She nods. Leans against my side, getting more comfortable. The server brings my drink. The pianist plays one of those melancholy tunes I've heard a million times but can't quite identify. We sip.

And when she sighs and rests her head against mine, I decide that my time has come. This conversation isn't going to get any easier.

"I think you're smart, Carly," I murmur. "Funny. Fascinating. Beautiful. *Sexy*. There's no one else like you. Never has been. Never could be."

A quick smile and wayward tear from her, which she quickly wipes away. She nods but says nothing.

"Since you're so fucking amazing, I can't believe I just happened to meet you. Or that you'd give me the time of day. Or that you're not already married to some old-money duke from back home. Or that you won't still decide that that's the kind of person you belong with."

She twists to face me. *"Damon —"*

"Shh." I squeeze her waist to make sure she understands how important this is. "I need you to *listen*. And it's hard enough to say this without you hitting me with those big baby blues."

The baby blues in question radiate steady warmth. Endless understanding. And I can't think with her looking at me like that.

Some of this must appear on my face, because she shows mercy on me and slowly faces the pianist again, waiting.

"I swing between thinking you want me for me and thinking you only want me for my money so you can rescue your precious father if he needs it or yourself if your art doesn't take off." I don't bother to hold back a self-deprecating laugh. "And not giving a damn if it *is* the money keeping you around. As long as you don't leave." I swallow hard, trying to get rid of the knot in my throat. "Like my mother left."

It feels like there should be more, but I can't think of it if there is.

"That it?" she asks crisply.

"That's it."

"Ask me how many fucks I give about your money," she says. "Go on. Ask me."

I open my mouth, but my voice struggles to keep up. Especially now that I'm beginning to feel sheepish.

"How many fucks do you give?" I ask quietly.

She twists again. Stares me in the face. "Zero."

Swear to God, I could drop to my knees and kiss her feet. That's how relieved I am by her ferocity.

"You sure about that, princess?"

"Zero."

Shaky laugh from me. Profound gratitude as I unwind my arm from around her waist and take her left hand in both of mine.

"I was hoping you'd say that," I tell her, laying her hand flat on my thigh and tracing letters on her palm.

I.

L. O. V. E.

Y. O. U.

My sweet princess laughs. Fails to stop a couple of crystalline tears from trickling down her face.

"I love you too," she whispers.

"I was hoping you'd say that again."

I reach into my pocket and find the ring I put there

earlier in an abundance of hope, place it in her palm and close her fingers around it.

She gasps and snatches her hand free so she can put the ring on the table and get a good look at it.

I'm no diamond expert. Just a guy who's got some money to throw around and the smarts to trust the experts at Harry Winston. Evidently, they know what they're doing, because she gasps at this thing—it's like a perfectly cut square ice cube—and can't hand it back to me fast enough.

I laugh.

"Thought you didn't care about the money," I say as I slide it on her finger.

"I can still tell you to fuck off if you try to get cheeky with me," she says, her severe warning look losing most of its teeth when she can't stop smiling.

"Wouldn't dream of it, princess."

The mood quickly shifts when she puts her hands on my face and gives me several hard kisses that make goosebumps race across my skin and tell me she means business.

"Take me upstairs," she says urgently.

"You got it."

We can't move fast enough. Luckily, I had the fore-sight—and that abundance of hope again—to book a suite earlier. By the time we hurry off the elevator and find our door, she can no longer keep her hands off me.

And thank God for that.

We reach for each other as I kick the door shut behind us, animals unleashed. It doesn't help that we've spent a few lonely nights apart while I came to my senses when normally we make love at least once a day. Our kisses are the deep, wet, frantic kind that lead to nips and bites. She wants to slide my jacket off my shoulders but first needs to wait for me to let go of her tight ass. She kicks off her heels. Reaches under her dress to wiggle her way out of her panties, then tosses them aside. I would dearly love to get rid of the rest of my clothes and, more importantly, her dress, but my dick can't wait that long.

Neither, it seems, can she.

She's already at work on my belt, undoing it and unzipping me while also somehow keeping hold of my waistband and tugging me down the hallway after her. Her fiery gaze stays locked on my face the entire time. The fact that she wants me a millionth as much as I want her feels like a miracle to me. If you'd told me a year ago that a woman like *this* was about to explode into my life, I would've laughed in your face.

But she's here. And she wants to stay.

She backs into the bed, then quickly reverses course and pushes *me* down on my back. Hey. Whatever works. I shimmy my pants and boxer briefs just far enough down my thighs to be out of our way. There's no time for anything else. She, meanwhile, shimmies her dress up to her hips, revealing that red patch of hair and the sweetest, hottest pussy in the world. Then she straddles me, and I take my dick in hand. But I pause at the last moment because something isn't right.

She frowns down at me, flustered and impatient. Just the way I like her.

"*What?*"

"What did I tell you about that hair?" I say.

She pauses, a sultry smile flickering across her face. Lets her head fall back as she finds the pin in her hair.

Pulls the pin out and shakes all that silky red goodness loose so it can drape around her face and shoulders.

Just the way I like it.

"Good girl," I say, holding my dick so she can impale herself on me.

Which she does without further delay.

Her slick heat sucks me in and grips me hard enough for the room to swim in and out of focus. We quickly find a driving rhythm, and she rides me hard with her hands on my chest, abandoned in her passion. There's something wildly illicit and intoxicating about seeing her like this, with her dress bunched up around her waist, her pale thighs flexing and her groin grinding against mine. Especially when she rears back and grips my ankles, a position that reveals the base of my dick, which is thick and ruddy inside her. I can't take my eyes off her flushed cheeks, her hair as it swings back and forth with her movements or the hard points of her nipples, which are still hidden by her dress but impossible to miss.

Equally mesmerizing? The way her expression shifts between smiles when we hit a spot she really likes and grimaces when we hit her sweet spot. And the way she mewls and pants and whispers to me, all of it encouraging me to fuck her harder. Faster.

I'm nothing if not a team player. My greedy hands fill themselves with her flexing thighs. Her swiveling hips. Her juicy ass. I give her everything I've got until my face is sweaty and her cries pitch higher as she straightens and puts her hands on her head as though she can't fucking stand it for another second.

And she can't, shouting out my name around her orgasm and stiffening as the pleasure possesses her. This is my cue to let myself go, which is a damn good thing, because I'm already going. She has a way of wrenching the pleasure from my body until I'm drained, then taking a little bit more and a little bit more. She's never satisfied until that moment where my vision fades, and the ecstasy is so sweet that I'd swear I have one foot in heaven. We ride it out together, our strangled cries giving way to lingering moans and then, finally, harsh breathing as air makes its way back into our lungs and she collapses on top of me.

Time passes. I don't know how much. Don't care. But at some point, she levers up enough to look down at my face. She's flushed. Amused. Gorgeous.

"Seems to me, this is where we came in," she says.

"There are some similarities," I say, anchoring my hand on her bare ass to keep her right where she is. "Only this time, you're not walking out on me. Are you?"

Glorious smile. "I am not."

"Good. Just to be clear, that's an engagement ring on your finger."

"Thank you for that clarification," she says, raising one delicate brow. "Since you haven't properly proposed. Nor have you been very abject in your apology, now that I think about it."

I can't hide my smirk.

"What can I say? I don't really do abject," I say, shrugging.

"No, you do not," she says sourly. "I can't help feeling I've let you off very easily."

"Sure you have," I say, dead serious as I stare her in the face. "If you consider me not being able to breathe days on end *easily*."

She leans down for a lingering kiss, looking mollified.

"But I can do the proposal. How's that?"

"Oh, by all means," she says eagerly, propping her head on her hand to watch me.

"Marry me, princess," I say, the words coming easily. As though they were there all along. As though I was born with them dormant inside me, waiting for this exact moment to bloom. "Don't make me try to live without you. We both know I can't do it."

Her smile is glorious enough to make everything inside me rejoice.

"I thought you'd never ask, my love."

"My love," I say, easing in for another kiss. "I like the sound of that. Make sure you keep using it."

"I plan to."

~

Keep reading for a special sneak peak of the second book in the series, Griffin's story,
***The Billionaire's Beauty*!**

EXCERPT FROM THE BILLIONAIRE'S BEAUTY

Chapter 1
Griffin

"About fucking time, Forest," I say.

I set my gin and tonic on the table and accept the thick envelope from my assistant, Bellamy Forest, when she arrives at my table. I'm enjoying celebratory drinks with my younger brother and business partner, Ryker, because we closed a big deal this afternoon. Our oldest brother, Damon, was also here, at least until he caught sight of some sultry redhead at another table a few minutes ago and took off for a closer look.

Bemelmans on the upper East Side isn't exactly the place for conducting business, especially with both the pianist and the crowd in full swing, but I need to spend a good chunk of my weekend reviewing these documents before the closing on Monday. Sucks for me, but it's tough out here for a real estate mogul who wants to stay on top of his game. True, I could have arranged for a courier to deliver the documents, but Bellamy is my right-hand person. One of the very few trustworthy people I know. Has been since the second she walked into my life a year ago. And she might as well earn the big bucks I pay her to keep my trains running on time. Even if it is both her twenty-sixth birthday and a Friday night, as evidenced by the spiky heels and little black dress she seems to be wearing under her blue shawl.

"Guess I'll cancel that missing persons report I just phoned in," I add.

An asshole comment? Of course. But I'm an asshole. Ask anyone. Luckily, Bellamy's salary includes a hardship premium for dealing with me and we've developed a system. I make a comment like that, she responds with a sarcastic little reminder of what a jackass I am, something like, "Sorry, Boss. Didn't realize there was traffic in Manhattan," and we keep it moving. I'm a busy guy. I don't have time to make friends. She understands that. That's why we get along so well professionally. We have our roles and we stick to them.

Which is why I'm surprised when she says the following:

"Sorry, Boss. Cops put a boot on my magic carpet. It was double-parked. Are we done here? I'd love to enjoy my twenty-sixth birthday before my twenty-seventh rolls around. Unless you plan to ruin my entire night."

I'd just tossed the envelope onto the table and started to reach for my drink again, but now I freeze. Exchange startled looks with my brother just to make sure I really heard that edgy tone coming from *her* mouth. Glance up and take a good look at Bellamy for the first time, wondering if I've been imagining the way she's gotten under my skin in the last several days.

Bellamy is crisp. She is cool. She is eminently professional. The thing she is not? Challenging. The thing she does not do? Make me think about her as a person.

As a woman.

But no, there it is. The veiled *What are you going to do about it?* in her stiff posture, squared shoulders and glinting brown eyes.

And, I gotta tell you, I find it fascinating.

One other thing I should mention? Bellamy Forest is easy on the eyes.

Look, I'm a heterosexual guy. I'm into women. Into everything about women. All women are beautiful.

But Bellamy Forest is *beautiful*. About average height, she's a perfect figure eight, with plenty of boobs in front, tons of ass out back and a tiny waist in between. She's *fit*, with toned legs and shoulders.

I love a fit woman.

And let's talk about her face for a minute. Big brown eyes, like I said. Cute little nose. X-rated mouth. English rose complexion. The kind of long and sun-kissed wavy brown hair that belongs in some glossy magazine ad for a high-end salon.

I'm not going to lie. I noticed all that about Bellamy the second she walked into my office for her interview a year ago. I also noticed her summa cum laude degree from Barnard College, her full-time gig as a tutor that helped her finance said degree and her ambition to work her amazing ass off and save money for law school. I can control my baser impulses when necessary, and it was necessary if I wanted to hire the best candidate for the job. Not to mention the fact that I don't want to get sued for sexual harassment. So I put my dick on lockdown, my attraction to her on a shelf and hired her.

Things have worked out great. Until now.

Now? My attraction is off that shelf. It didn't ask for my permission to jump down. It just did. And my dick is starting to seriously resent the lockdown.

"Actually, we're *not* done." I stare her dead in the face, eager to see what she'll do next. Not a good idea, for which I partially blame this second gin and tonic. "I'm going to need you for a bit longer tonight. You might want to let your friends know you'll be late."

Confession: I went to the office kitchen earlier for a cup of coffee, during which time I overheard Bellamy discussing tonight's plans with another staffer that she's friendly with. Naturally, they hushed up when I walked into the room, but not before I heard mention of drinks, dinner, a club and some sexy guy everyone wants Bellamy to meet. Not that anyone asked my opinion, but I was fine with all of it. Until I heard about this sexy guy. The idea of Bellamy hooking up with some faceless sexy guy rubs me the wrong way.

Matter of fact, it rubs me so wrong that it wrecked most of my afternoon while I tried to convince myself that I'm not jealous.

This was an unexpected and unwelcome development. I can't figure out when things went sideways on me. Can't stop wishing I could get this runaway genie back in the bottle.

Don't get me wrong. Bellamy is a grown woman. I'm sure she's had sex since she joined my company's payroll. I never thought about it. Never cared. Until this afternoon, when the information about her personal life whacked me on the back of the head like a nail-studded two by four swung by Barry Bonds.

The bottom line? I don't like the idea of my Bellamy (not that she's *my* Bellamy, but you know what I mean) spending her birthday fucking some loser, and I'm not crying over the fact that I have the power to put the kibosh on those plans, at least temporarily.

I'm not crying at all.

She blinks. Reins in her frown with what looks like a significant amount of effort. "How late?"

"Hard to say," I say, shrugging. "Will that be a problem?"

To her credit, she manages a smile. A crooked smile, but still credible.

"Not at all," she says, glancing around just as a nearby couple get up and leave their table. "Why don't I just sit over there since there's no room at this table? Damon. Ryker. Hope you two have a great night."

"Hope you get to enjoy what's left of your birthday, Bellamy," Ryker says.

"Don't let him give you too much shit, Bellamy," Damon tells her.

"Don't worry," she says, laughing. "I've got this."

With that, she turns to go while also unwrapping that blue shawl and giving me a spectacular and mouthwatering view of the body she normally keeps tucked inside her business attire. Tonight? It's poured into a little black dress with heavy emphasis on *little*. It's got no sleeves. No nothing other than a stretchy tube that bares a fair amount of cleavage before clinging to her hips and ass and trailing off well before it hits her knees. But before I can lament the fact that I can't see much of her legs, she takes another step, revealing a slit and a juicy stretch of thigh.

The sort of thigh a man wants wrapped around his waist when he's buried deep inside a gorgeous woman.

I'm not shitting you when I say that the sight of that

glowing skin, shifting hair and insane figure is like a lightning strike to my entire existence.

My head commands me not to do anything stupid. My dick commands me to fuck her as soon as possible. Something deep inside me—trapped somewhere between my chest and my gut—wonders what the *fuck* is happening to my world tonight.

My turmoil is intensified when she glances back over her shoulder and gives me just enough of a lingering look for me to wonder if she wants me to come hither.

Or maybe that's just my runaway hormones projecting things onto her.

Doesn't matter. I'm already on my feet, determined to follow her like a heat seeking missile…

If you enjoyed this excerpt, grab *The Billionaire's Beauty* now! And don't forget the final book in the series, Ryker's story, *The Billionaire's Cinderella*!

ALSO BY AVA RYAN

Fairy Tale Billionaires Series

The Billionaire's Princess

The Billionaire's Beauty

The Billionaire's Cinderella

To DH
XOXO

ACKNOWLEDGMENTS

Special thanks to Nina Grinstead and the team at Grey's Promotions for helping me launch this baby and to Croco Designs for the lovely covers. Big thanks to my writer friends for holding my hand and/or talking me down from ledges as needed. You know who you are. Hopefully, you also know how much I love you.

ABOUT THE AUTHOR

Ava Ryan is an author of sexy contemporary romance. Her favorite things, in no special order, are animals, her family, cookies, people with great senses of humor and love stories. Currently in her writer's cave (ostensibly working hard on her next book while also checking Netflix every few hours to make sure she hasn't missed a new true crime documentary show), she loves hearing from readers via her website or social media.

If you love billionaire alpha males, the feisty women who snag their hearts and books that end with a happily ever after, you've come to the right place.

Please make sure to Subscribe to Ava's VIP List to stay in the loop about her latest releases and upcoming books.

Finally, don't forget to follow her on BookBub to learn about any special promotions on her books.